Excerpts fro

From "The Storyteller"

Bertha saw the wolf creeping toward her, and she wished she had never been invited to the park. She ran as fast as she could, but the wolf came after her with huge leaps and bounds.

From "The Ransom of Red Chief"

At daybreak I was woken up by awful screams from Bill. . . . I jumped up to see what the matter was. Red Chief was sitting on Bill's chest, pulling a handful of his hair. In his other hand he had the sharp knife we used for slicing bacon. He was really trying to take Bill's scalp, like he had threatened the night before.

From "The Open Window"

The girl stared out the window with horror in her eyes. Chilled by fear, Framton turned around and looked out the window.

LAUGHTER AND CHILLS

SEVEN GREAT STORIES

Edited by
Anne G. Crocco, Martin E. Goldstein,
David Kleiner, and Beth Johnson

Afterword by Beth Johnson

 THE TOWNSEND LIBRARY

LAUGHTER AND CHILLS:
SEVEN GREAT STORIES

TP **THE TOWNSEND LIBRARY**

For more titles in the Townsend Library,
visit our website: **www.townsendpress.com**

Townsend Press, Inc.
1038 Industrial Drive
West Berlin, New Jersey 08091

ISBN 1-59194-040-0

Library of Congress Control Number:
2004099156

CONTENTS

PREVIEW

When three children
are trapped on a long
journey with their
aunt, a boring
storyteller, a stranger
comes to their aid. Is
the stranger a hero or
a villain? It depends on
who you ask—the
children or their aunt!

THE STORYTELLER
Saki

It was a hot afternoon, and inside the train it was steamy. The next stop was Templecombe, which was almost an hour ahead. In one car of the train there were a little girl, an even younger girl, and a little boy. Their aunt sat in a seat in the corner. In the opposite corner of the car was a bachelor who didn't know them. The girls and the boy were all over the train car. The aunt kept telling the children "Don't," while the children kept asking her questions starting with "Why?" The bachelor said nothing to them.

"Don't, Cyril, don't!" exclaimed the aunt, as the boy began hitting the seat cushions, making clouds of dust fly up. "Come over here and look out the window."

Reluctantly, the boy went over to the window. "Why are they driving those sheep out of that field?" he asked.

"I guess they are being taken to another field that has more grass," said the aunt weakly.

"But there's lots of grass in that field," protested the boy. "There's nothing but grass there. Aunt, there's **lots** of grass in that field."

"Maybe the grass in the other field is better," the aunt suggested foolishly.

"Why is it better?" came the quick, obvious question.

"Oh, look at those cows!" exclaimed the aunt. Almost every field they passed was full of cows and bulls, but she acted like it was an unusual thing.

"Why is the grass in the other field better?" Cyril kept at her.

The frown on the bachelor's face was deepening into a scowl. The aunt saw him and decided he was a mean, unfriendly man. And she couldn't come up with any good explanation for the little boy about the grass in the field.

The younger girl tried to entertain herself

and everyone else by starting to recite a poem. She only knew the first line, but she used that as much as possible. She repeated the line over and over again in a dreamy but loud voice. The bachelor thought it seemed like someone had bet her she couldn't say that same line two thousand times without stopping. Unfortunately for him, it seemed like she was going to win the bet.

"Come over here and listen to a story," said the aunt, when the bachelor had given her two nasty looks and looked like he was going to call the train conductor.

The children moved over toward the aunt without any enthusiasm. They obviously did not think the aunt was a very good storyteller.

In a quiet voice that was often interrupted by loud questions from the children, the aunt started a not-so-interesting story about a little girl who was good. Because she was so good, she made a lot of friends, and was finally saved from a wild bull by people who admired how good she was.

"Would they have saved her if she hadn't been good?" demanded the older of the little girls. That was exactly the question the bachelor wanted to ask.

"Well, yes," answered the aunt lamely, "but I don't think they would have run so fast to help her if they hadn't liked her so much."

"It's the stupidest story I've ever heard," said the older of the little girls.

"I didn't even listen after the first part because it was so stupid," said Cyril.

The younger girl didn't comment on the story, but long before she had stopped listening and started repeating the line from the poem again.

"You don't seem to be a very good story-teller," said the bachelor suddenly.

The aunt immediately got defensive at this unexpected attack. "It's very difficult to tell stories that children will understand and enjoy," she said stiffly.

"I don't agree with you," said the bachelor.

"Maybe you'd like to tell them a story," the aunt shot back.

"Tell us a story!" demanded the older of the little girls.

"Once upon a time," began the bachelor, "there was a little girl called Bertha, who was very, very good."

The children's temporary interest started fading immediately. To them, all stories seemed boring and the same, no matter who told them.

"She did everything she was told to do. She always told the truth and kept her clothes neat and clean. She ate food that was good for her instead of junk food and sweets, got good grades in school, and was polite to everyone."

"Was she pretty?" asked the older little girl.

"Not as pretty as any of you," said the bachelor, "but she was horribly good."

The children showed they liked this part of the story; the word horrible in connection with goodness was something new and they liked it. It seemed real and true, unlike the aunt's stories about children.

"She was so good," continued the bachelor, "that she won several medals for goodness, which she always wore, pinned to her dress. There was a medal for following rules, one for being on time, and one for general good behavior. They were large metal medals and they clicked against each other when she walked. No other child in her town had three medals, so everyone knew that she must be an extra good child."

"Horribly good," repeated Cyril.

"Everybody talked about how good she was, and the Prince of the country heard about it. He decided she was so good that he would let her walk once a week in his park just outside the town. It was a beautiful park, and no children had ever been allowed in it before. So it was a great honor for Bertha to be allowed to go there."

"Were there any sheep in the park?" demanded Cyril.

"No," said the bachelor, "there were no sheep."

"Why weren't there any sheep?" came the unavoidable question.

The aunt had a big smile on her face.

"There were no sheep in the park," said the bachelor, "because the Prince's mother had once had a dream that her son would either be killed by a sheep or by a clock falling on him. So the Prince never kept sheep in his park or a clock in his palace."

The aunt gasped in admiration at how well the bachelor had answered the question.

"Was the Prince killed by a sheep or a clock?" asked Cyril.

"He is still alive, so we don't know if the dream will come true," said the bachelor. "Anyway, there were no sheep in the park, but there were lots of little pigs running all over the place."

"What color were they?"

"Black with white faces, white with black spots, black all over, gray with white patches, and some were white all over."

The storyteller stopped to let the children imagine all of the great things about the park, and then started again: "Bertha was sad to find that there were no flowers in the park. With tears in her eyes she had promised her aunts that she wouldn't pick any of the flowers. She wanted to keep her promise, and it made her feel silly that there weren't any flowers to pick."

"Why weren't there any flowers?"

"Because the pigs had eaten all of them," said the bachelor right away. "The gardeners told the Prince he couldn't have both pigs and flowers, so he decided to keep the pigs and forget the flowers."

The children were all happy with the Prince's choice; so many people would have picked the flowers over the pigs.

"There were lots of other fun things in the park. There were ponds with gold, blue, and green fish in them, and trees with beautiful talking parrots, and hummingbirds that could hum popular music. Bertha walked around and totally enjoyed herself. She thought, 'If I weren't so very good, they wouldn't have let me come to this beautiful park and enjoy everything in it.' Her three medals clinked against each other as she walked and again reminded her how good she was. But then a very big wolf came into the park to hunt for a fat little pig for its supper."

"What color was it?" asked the children, who were now very interested in the story.

"Mud colored all over, with a black tongue and fierce pale gray eyes. The first thing it saw in the park was Bertha. Her white dress was so spotlessly white and clean that you could see it from far away. Bertha saw the wolf creeping toward her, and she wished she had never been invited to the park. She ran as fast as she could, but the wolf came after her with huge leaps and bounds. She managed to reach some bushes and she hid in them. The wolf sniffed the bushes and she could see its black tongue hanging out of its mouth and its angry gray eyes. Bertha was very scared, and thought, 'If I had not been so very good, I would be safe back in town right now.'

"However, the smell of the bushes was so strong and the branches were so thick that the wolf couldn't smell or see Bertha, so it decided to go catch a pig instead. Bertha was so scared of the wolf that she was shaking and her medals for goodness started clinking together. The wolf was just moving away when it heard the medals clinking and stopped to listen. When they clinked again in a bush near him, it dove into the bush with its gray eyes shining fiercely. It dragged Bertha out and ate her all up. All that was left were her shoes, pieces of clothing, and the three medals for goodness."

"Were any of the pigs killed?"

"No, they all escaped."

"The story started badly," said the younger girl, "but it had a beautiful ending."

"It is the most beautiful story I have ever heard," said the older little girl seriously.

"It is the *only* beautiful story I have ever heard," said Cyril.

The aunt disagreed. "That is an inappropriate story to tell young children! You will undo years of careful teaching."

"Anyway," said the bachelor, getting his stuff together so he could get off the train. "I kept them quiet for ten minutes, which was more than you could do."

"Poor woman!" he thought to himself as he walked down the platform of Templecombe station. "For the next six months those children will beg her in public for an inappropriate story!"

PREVIEW

Mix together two
not-so-dangerous
criminals, a "two-
legged skyrocket"
of a boy, and a father
who knows his son
all too well. The result
is a kidnapping that
goes wrong in all the
right ways.

THE RANSOM OF RED CHIEF

O'Henry

It looked like a good thing: but wait till I tell you. We were down South, in Alabama—Bill Driscoll and myself—when we got this kidnapping idea. It was, as Bill said afterward, "during a moment of temporary insanity"; but we didn't find that out till later.

There was a town down there in Alabama, as flat as a pancake but called Summit, of course. The people who lived there were as happy and unthreatening a group of hillbillies as you could ever meet.

Between us, Bill and me had about six hundred dollars, and we needed just two thousand dollars more to pull off a real estate scam in Western Illinois. We talked it over on the front steps of the hotel. Loving your kids, says we, is big in these small towns. A kidnapping project should do better here than in cities which have a lot of cops and news reporters stirring things up. We knew that Summit only had a very small police force and a little weekly farmers' newspaper. So it looked good.

For our victim we picked the only child of a well-known citizen named Ebenezer Dorset. As a father, Dorset was respectable and strict, and he was a mortgage broker who was serious about collecting debts. The kid was a ten-year-old boy with freckles and flaming red hair. Bill and me figured that Ebenezer would give up a ransom of two thousand dollars for him. But wait till I tell you.

About two miles from Summit was a little mountain, thickly covered with pine trees. In back of the mountain was a cave, where we stored our food and our stuff.

One evening after sunset, we drove a rented car past old Dorset's house. The kid was in the street, throwing rocks at a kitten by the fence across the street.

"Hey little boy!" says Bill. "Would you like some candy and to go for a ride?"

The boy hit Bill right in the eye with a piece of brick.

"That will cost the old man an extra five hundred dollars," says Bill, getting out of the car.

The boy fought like a big brown bear, but at last we got him into the car and drove away. We took him up to the cave and parked the car in the trees. When it was totally dark I drove the car back to the rental place three miles away and walked back to the mountain.

Bill was patching up the scratches and bruises on his face. There was a fire burning behind the big rock at the entrance of the cave, and the boy was watching a pot of boiling coffee, with two buzzard tail feathers stuck in his red hair. He points a stick at me when I come in, and says:

"Ha! Paleface, do you dare to enter the camp of Red Chief, the terror of the plains?"

"He's all right now," says Bill, rolling up his pants to look at some bruises on his legs. "We're playing Indian. We're wilder than all of the old Wild West movies. I'm Old Hank, the Trapper, Red Chief's prisoner, and he'll scalp me at daybreak. Wow, that kid can kick hard."

Yes sir, that boy seemed to be having the time of his life. The fun of camping out in a cave seemed to make him forget that he was the one who was really the prisoner. He gave me the name Snake-Eye, the Spy, and announced that when the other Indians returned from the

warpath I would be burned at the stake at sunrise.

Then we had supper. With his mouth full of
bacon, bread, and gravy, he started talking non-
stop: "I like this. I never camped out before, but
I had a pet possum once, and I was nine on my
last birthday. I hate to go to school. Rats ate up
sixteen of Jimmy Talbot's aunt's hen's eggs. Are
there any real Indians in these woods? I want
some more gravy. Does the trees moving make
the wind blow? We had five puppies. What
makes your nose so red, Hank? My father has
lots of money. Are the stars hot? I beat up Ed
Walker twice on Saturday. I don't like girls. You
need a string to catch frogs. Do bulls make any
noise? Why are oranges round? Do we have any
beds to sleep on in this cave? Amos Murray has
six toes. A parrot can talk, but a monkey and a
fish can't. How many does it take to make
twelve?"

Every few minutes he would remember he
was an Indian, and would pick up his stick used
as a gun and tiptoe to the front of the cave to
look out for palefaces. Now and then he would
give a war cry that made Old Hank the Trapper
shiver. That boy had Bill afraid of him from the
start.

"Red Chief," says I to the kid, "would you
like to go home?"

"Aw, what for?" says he. "I don't have any

fun at home. I hate to go to school. I like to camp out. You won't take me home again, Snake-eye, will you?"

"Not right away," says I. "We'll stay here in the cave awhile."

"All right!" he says. "That'll be great. I never had so much fun in my life."

We went to bed around eleven o'clock. We spread out some big blankets and quilts and put Red Chief between us. We weren't afraid he would run away. He kept us awake for three hours, jumping up and reaching for his stick gun and yelling, "Hey, pardner!" in my and Bill's ears when he heard a leaf move or stick crack and imagined it was a group of outlaws. Finally I fell asleep and slept restlessly, dreaming I had been kidnapped and chained to a tree by a fierce pirate with red hair.

At daybreak I was woken up by awful screams from Bill. They weren't the yells or shouts of a man; they were terrifying, humiliating screams like women make when they see ghosts or caterpillars. It is an awful thing to hear a strong but desperate fat man scream in a cave in the morning.

I jumped up to see what the matter was. Red Chief was sitting on Bill's chest, pulling a handful of his hair. In his other hand he had the sharp knife we used for slicing bacon. He was really trying to take Bill's scalp, like he had threatened the night before.

I got the knife away from the kid and made him lie down again. But from that moment, Bill's spirit was broken. He lay down on the side of the bed, but he wouldn't close his eyes again as long as the boy was with us. I dozed off for a while, but then I remembered that Red Chief had said I would be burned at the stake at the rising of the sun. I wasn't nervous or afraid, but I sat up and lit my pipe and leaned against a rock.

"Why are you getting up so early, Sam?" asked Bill.

"Me?" says I. "Oh, I got a kind of pain in my shoulder. I thought sitting up would rest it."

"You're a liar!" says Bill. "You're afraid that he'll really try to burn you at sunrise. He would, too, if he could find a match. Ain't it awful, Sam? Do you think anybody will pay money to get that little devil back home?"

"Sure," I said. "A rowdy kid like that is just the kind parents are crazy about. Now, you and the Chief get up and cook breakfast, while I go up to the top of the mountain to look around."

I climbed to the top of the little mountain and looked out over the area. Over toward Summit I expected to see the people of the village armed with guns and knives looking for the dangerous kidnappers. All I saw was a peaceful landscape with one farmer plowing his field.

Nobody was searching the creek for bodies; nobody was running around, looking for news for the upset parents. All I saw was the sleepy countryside of Alabama. I says to myself, "Maybe nobody has discovered that the wolves have stolen the little sheep. Heaven help the wolves!" And I went down for breakfast.

When I got to the cave, I found Bill backed up against one of the walls, breathing hard, with the boy threatening to smash him with a rock almost the size of a coconut.

"He put a red-hot potato down my back," explained Bill, "and then mashed it with his foot, so I slapped him. Do you have a gun, Sam?"

I took the rock away from the boy and tried to get them to make up. "I'll get you," says the kid to Bill. "No man ever hit the Red Chief and got away with it. You better watch out!"

After breakfast the kid took a piece of leather with strings wrapped around it out of his pocket and walked out of the cave, unwinding it.

"What's he up to now?" asks Bill, worried. "You don't think he'll run away, do you Sam?'

"No way," says I. "He doesn't seem like a kid who likes to be home. But we've got to get the plan straight about the ransom. There doesn't seem to be much excitement around Summit about his disappearance, but maybe they haven't figured out that he's gone yet. His parents may think he's spending the night with a relative or one of the neighbors. Anyhow, they'll miss him today. Tonight we have to get a message to his father demanding two thousand dollars to give him back."

Just then we heard a kind of a war-whoop. It was a sling that Red Chief had pulled out of his pocket, and he was whirling it around his head.

I ducked, and heard a big bump and a cry from Bill. A rock the size of an egg had hit Bill just behind his left ear. He fell into the campfire and knocked over a frying pan full of hot water for washing the dishes. I dragged him out and poured cold water over his head for half an hour.

Eventually, Bill woke up and says, "You won't go away and leave me here alone, will you Sam?"

I went out, caught the boy, and shook him until his freckles rattled. "If you don't behave," says I, "I'll take you straight home. Now, are you going to be good, or not?"

"I was only having fun," says he, sounding grumpy. "I didn't mean to hurt Old Hank. But why did he hit me? I'll behave, Snake-eye, if you won't send me home, and if you'll let me play the Black Scout today."

"I don't know that game," I says. "That's for you and Mr. Bill to decide. He'll play with

you all day. I'm going away for a while, on business. Now, come in, make friends and say you're
sorry for hurting him, or you'll go home right
now."

I made him and Bill shake hands, and then
I took Bill aside and told him I was going to
Poplar Cove, a little town three miles from the
cave, to find out what people were saying about
the kidnapping in Summit. Also, I thought it
would be a good idea to send the first letter to
old man Dorset that day, demanding the ransom
and telling how he should pay it.

"You know, Sam," says Bill, "I've stood by
you with no fear in earthquakes, fires, floods,
poker games, explosions, police raids, train rob-
beries, and tornados. I never lost my nerve till
we kidnapped that two-legged skyrocket of a
kid. He's driving me crazy. You won't leave me
alone with him for long, will you Sam?"

"I'll be back some time this afternoon," says
I. "You must keep the boy happy and quiet until
I come back. And now we'll write the letter to
Old Dorset."

Bill and I got a pencil and paper and worked
on the letter while Red Chief, with a blanket
wrapped around him, marched up and down,
guarding the mouth of the cave. Bill begged me
with tears in his eyes to make the ransom fifteen
hundred instead of two thousand. He said, "I
ain't trying to put down the importance of a

parent's love for his child, but we're dealing with humans. It ain't human for anybody to give up two thousand dollars for that freckled wildcat. I'm willing to take a chance and ask for fifteen hundred dollars. You can charge the other five hundred to me."

To make Bill feel better, I gave in, and we worked together on this letter:

> Dear Mr. Ebenezer Dorset:
>
> We have your son hidden in a place far from Summit. There is no way you or even the best detectives could find him. This is the only way you can get him back: At midnight tonight, leave fifteen hundred dollars in large bills at the place we will describe. If you agree to this deal, send one person with an answer to that spot tonight at 8:30. To get to the drop-off place for the reply and the money, take the road to Poplar Cove and cross Owl Creek. There are three large trees close to a fence by a wheat field. At the bottom of the fence opposite the third tree will be a small cardboard box. Have your messenger drop your answer in this box and then return to Summit.
>
> If you try any tricks or do not do what we ask, you will never see your son again. If you give us the money we ask for, we will return him safely within three hours. This is our final offer, and your only chance. We will not send another letter.
>
> Signed, TWO DESPERATE MEN

I addressed the letter to Dorset and put it in my pocket. As I was about to leave, the kid came up to me and said, "Aw, Snake-Eye, you said I could play the Black Scout while you were gone."

"You can play Black Scout," says I. "Mr. Bill will play it with you. How do you play?"

"I'm the Black Scout," the Red Chief says, "and I have to ride to the fort to warn the settlers that the Indians are coming. I'm tired of pretending I am the Indian. I want to be the Black Scout."

"OK," I says. "It sounds harmless. I guess Mr. Bill will help you fight the Indians."

"What do I have to do?" Bill asks, looking suspiciously at the kid.

"You are my horse," says Black Scout. "Get down on your hands and knees. How can I ride to the fort without a horse?"

"You better keep him entertained until we get the plan in motion," I said. "Loosen up."

Bill gets down on his hands and knees, his eyes looking like a rabbit's in a trap. "How far is it to the fort, kid?"

"Ninety miles," says the Black Scout. "You better gallop to get there on time. Giddy-up!" The Black Scout jumps on Bill's back and digs his heels into his side.

Bill says, "Sam, you better hurry back as soon as you can. I wish we hadn't made the ransom more than a thousand. Hey, quit kicking me or I'll get up and beat you."

I walked over to Poplar Cove and sat around the local post office and store, talking with the local shoppers. One old guy says he hears that Summit was all upset because Ebenezer Dorset's boy had disappeared. That was all I wanted to know. I bought some pipe tobacco, casually mailed the letter, and left. The guy at the post office said the mailman would come by in an hour to take the mail to Summit.

When I got back to the cave, I couldn't find Bill and the boy. I looked all around and called their names a couple of times, but they didn't answer. So I lit my pipe and sat down to wait for something to happen.

In about half an hour, I heard a sound in the bushes, and Bill came through the opening in the woods. Behind him was the kid, tiptoeing silently like a scout, smiling. Bill stopped, took off his hat and wiped his face with a red hand-kerchief. The kid stopped about eight feet behind him.

"Sam," says Bill, "you may think I am a trai-tor, but I couldn't help it. I'm a grown man who can defend myself, but there is a time when everything else fails. The boy is gone; I sent him home and the kidnapping is off. In the old days, there were martyrs that would rather die than give up the money they were after. But none of them were ever tortured the way I have been. I tried to stay true to our plan, but I reached my limit."

"What happened, Bill?"

"He rode me," says Bill, "the whole ninety miles to the fort. After we rescued the settlers, he gave me 'oats'. Sand tastes horrible! And then, for an hour I had to explain why holes have nothing in them, how a road works both ways and what makes grass green. I tell you, Sam, a human can only stand so much. I grabbed him by the back of the neck and dragged him down the mountain. On the way, he kicked my legs black-and-blue from the knees down, and I've got two or three bites on my hand."

"But he's gone," Bill continues. "Gone home. I showed him the road to Summit and gave him a kick to get him started. I'm sorry we won't get the ransom money, but it was either the money or me going crazy."

Bill was breathing hard, but his face looked peaceful and happy.

"Bill," says I, "there isn't any heart disease in your family, is there?"

"No," says Bill. "Just malaria and accidents. Why?"

"Then maybe you should turn around and look behind you," I says.

Bill turned and saw the boy, and grew pale

and flopped on the ground, picking sadly at sticks and grass. For an hour I thought he was losing his mind. Then I told him my plan was already happening and that we would have the money and leave by midnight if old Dorset fell for it. So Bill got himself together enough to give the kid a weak smile and he agreed to play soldiers with him as soon as he felt a little better.

I had a plan for getting the ransom money without getting caught. The tree with the box for the answer and the money had big, bare fields on all sides, so I couldn't sneak up on it because you could see the spot from far away. So I got there early and climbed the tree before anyone could see me, and waited for the messenger to show up.

Exactly on time, an older boy rode up on a bicycle, put a slip of folded paper into the cardboard box and rode away again toward Summit. I waited an hour and then decided it was safe. I slid down the tree, got the note, and was back in the cave in a half an hour. I opened the note and read it to Bill by flashlight. The letter said:

> **Dear Two Desperate Men:**
> In the mail today I got your letter about the ransom for the return of my son. I think you are asking too much, so here is my counter-offer, which I think you will accept. You bring Johnny home and pay *me* two hundred and fifty dollars in cash, and I agree to take him off

your hands. You better come at night, because
the neighbors think he is lost, and I can't be
responsible for what they would do to anyone
who they saw bringing him back.

Sincerely, Ebenezer Dorset

"No way! Of all the rude…" I start to say.

But I looked at Bill, and stopped. His eyes
were begging me. He says, "Sam, what's two
hundred and fifty dollars after all? We've got the
money. One more night with this kid and I'll be
in the mental hospital. Besides being a gentleman, I think Mr. Dorset is very generous to
make us this offer. You ain't going to give up
this chance, are you?"

"To tell you the truth, Bill," says I, "this little lamb has gotten on my nerves a little, too.
We'll take him home, pay the ransom, and make
our getaway."

We took him home that night. We got him
to go by telling him his father had a gun and a
pair of moccasins for him, and that we were
going to hunt bears the next day.

It was just midnight when we knocked on
Ebenezer's front door. At the exact moment we
should have been getting fifteen hundred dollars out of our box under the tree, Bill was
counting out two hundred and fifty dollars into
Dorset's hand. When the kid found out we were
going to leave him at home he started howling
like a wolf, and grabbed onto Bill's leg. His
father had to slowly peel him off.

"How long can you hold him?" asks Bill.

"I'm not as strong as I used to be," old Dorset said, "but I think I can promise you ten minutes."

"That will do," says Bill. "In ten minutes I will be half way to Canada."

As dark as it was, and as fat as Bill was, and as good a runner as I am, he was more than a mile and a half out of Summit before I could catch up with him.

PREVIEW

It's a lovely autumn afternoon in a peaceful house in the country. It seems like the perfect place for Framton Nuttel to rest and relax after an illness. There's just one problem: an open window that his fifteen-year-old hostess expects three dead men to walk through. . . .

THE OPEN WINDOW

Saki

"My aunt will come downstairs soon, Mr. Nuttel," said a very self-confident fifteen-year-old girl. "While we are waiting, you must try and put up with me."

Framton Nuttel tried to think of something to say that would entertain the niece at that moment without offending the aunt who would soon be there. He was making a series of visits to total strangers because his doctors told him that it would help cure his nerves, but he doubted it would really work.

"I know what will happen," his sister had said when he was getting ready to go away to the country. "You will bury yourself there and not talk to anyone, and then your nerves will be worse than ever from moping. I will give you letters so you can introduce yourself to people I knew there. As far as I can remember, some of them are very nice."

Framton wondered whether Mrs. Sappleton, the lady he was meeting today, was one of the nice people she remembered.

"Do you know many of the people around here?" asked the niece, when she got tired of sitting in silence with the visitor.

"Hardly anyone," said Framton. "My sister stayed in this area four years ago, and she gave me letters to introduce me to some of the people here," he said, sounding like he wished she hadn't.

"Then you don't really know anything about my aunt?" pursued the confident young lady.

"Only her name and address," admitted the visitor. He was wondering if Mrs. Sappleton was married or widowed. The decorations in the room made him think a man lived there.

"Three years ago a terrible tragedy happened to her," said the girl. "It happened after your sister lived here."

"A tragedy?" asked Framton. Somehow, in this peaceful country spot, tragedies seemed out of place.

"You may wonder why we keep that window wide open on an October afternoon," said the niece, pointing to a large French window that opened onto the back yard.

"It's warm for October," said Framton, "but does the window have anything to do with the tragedy?"

"Three years ago today, my aunt's husband and her two young brothers left through that window to go hunting. They never came back. While crossing a field to their favorite bird hunting spot, they were all drowned in a dangerous swampy hole. It had rained a lot that summer, and places that were safe in other years gave way suddenly without warning. We never found their bodies. That was the terrible part about it." At this point, the girl's voice became less confident and sounded sad and shaky. "Poor Aunt always thinks they will come back some day with the little brown dog that was lost with them, and that they will walk back in through that big window like they used to. That's why the window is kept open each evening until it is dark. My poor dear aunt often tells me how they went out, her husband with his white raincoat over his arm, and her youngest brother Ronnie singing 'Bertie, Why Do You Bound?'. He always sang that to tease her, because it got on her nerves. You know, sometimes on calm, quiet evenings like this, I almost get the creepy feeling that they will all walk in through that window…"

She stopped with a shiver. Framton was relieved when the aunt hurried into the room, apologizing for taking so long.

"I hope my niece Vera has been entertaining you?" she said.

"She has been very interesting," said Framton.

"I hope you don't mind the open window," said Mrs. Sappleton quickly and cheerfully. "Soon my husband and brothers will be home from hunting, and they always come in this way. They've been out bird hunting near the swamps, so they will get their muddy feet all over the carpets. That's how you men are, isn't it?"

She kept talking cheerfully about hunting, how few birds there were, and about how many ducks there would be that winter. To Framton it was totally horrible. He tried desperately to change the subject. He noticed that the aunt was only partly paying attention to him, and kept looking out the window into the yard. It was a terrible coincidence that he was visiting on the anniversary of the tragedy.

Framton tried to change the subject by talking about his illness. "The doctors all say I need complete rest, with no strenuous exercise and no emotional excitement." Like many people, he thought total strangers would be interested in all of the details of his medical condition. "However, they can't agree on what kind of diet I should be on."

"They can't?" said Mrs. Sappleton, who talked to stop from yawning. Then suddenly she looked happy and alert—but not from what Framton was saying.

"Finally they are here!" she cried. "Just in time for tea, and covered with mud!"

Framton shivered and turned toward the niece with a look to show her he knew what was happening to her aunt, and that he was sorry for her. The girl stared out the window with horror in her eyes. Chilled by fear, Framton turned around and looked out the window.

It was getting dark, and three people were walking across the lawn toward the window. They all carried guns and one had a white raincoat. A tired brown dog followed them closely. They were silent, but as they got close to the house a young voice sang, "I said, Bertie, where are you bound?"

Framton wildly grabbed his hat and ran out the front door, up the driveway, and out the front gate. A person riding down the road on a bike crashed into a bush to avoid running into him.

"We're home, my dear," said the man in the white raincoat, coming in through the big back window. "We got muddy, but most of it is dry now. Who was that who ran out as we came in?"

"A very strange man named Mr. Nuttel," said Mrs. Sappleton. "All he did was talk about his illness and then ran off without saying sorry or good-bye when you came in. He acted like he had seen a ghost."

"I bet it was the brown dog," said the niece calmly. "He told me he was afraid of dogs. He told me he was once in India and a pack of wild dogs chased him into a cemetery. He had to spend the night down in a newly dug grave with the dogs snarling and barking at him from above. That would be enough to make anyone lose their nerve."

Drama at the drop of a hat was her specialty.

PREVIEW

"No one injures me and gets away with it." Although we never know just how Fortunato has offended this story's narrator, we soon learn just how serious the narrator is. If you think the jingle of bells is a pleasant sound, you may not after finishing this tale.

Note about "The Cask of Amontillado"

This story is set during the festival known as Carnival. Celebrated in many countries, Carnival is the time of merry-making that occurs before Lent (the forty days before Easter). During Lent, many Christians pray, reflect, and even give up eating meat. Carnival, which means "farewell to meat" in Latin, is a last fling before the start of Lent. Eating, drinking, and the wearing of costumes all add to the party atmosphere.

THE CASK OF AMONTILLADO

Edgar Allan Poe

I must have put up with Fortunato's abuses a thousand times. But when he started insulting me, I swore revenge. You know me well enough to appreciate that I never threatened him to his face. I knew that, sooner or later, I would get him back. That was certain. In fact, my desire for revenge was so strong, I had to be that much more careful to avoid giving myself away. Fortunato must not find out what I had in mind, yet. Later, when he clearly understood who was doing him wrong, my revenge would be complete.

Nothing I did ever gave Fortunato cause to doubt my friendliness. I continued to smile—as I always had—whenever I saw him. How could he know I was smiling this time at the thought of his murder?

Fortunato was a man to be respected and even feared. But he had one weakness. He fancied himself a great expert on wine. In other things, like art and gems, he would fake enthusiasm to impress you. But when it came to wine, his passion was sincere. In this respect, Fortunato and I were alike. I knew the finest Italian vintages, and bought great quantities whenever I could.

One evening during the wild partying of Carnival, I happened to meet Fortunato. He greeted me with excessive friendliness, for he'd had too much to drink. I acted so pleased to see him, I thought I'd never finish shaking his hand. He was wearing a costume for Carnival. How fitting! The fool had chosen the multi-colored suit and cap and bells of a jester.

I said, "My dear Fortunato, you look well today. And how lucky that I ran into you. I just bought a full cask of what is supposed to be the finest Amontillado wine. But I have my doubts."

"What?" he said. "Amontillado in that quantity? At this time of year? Impossible!"

"How silly of me to pay the full Amon–tillado price without consulting you. But I was afraid I'd miss my chance."

"Amontillado!"

"I have my doubts."

"Amontillado!"

"I've got to find out if it really is...but, you're busy and I'm on my way to see Luchresi. He is a true expert. If anyone can tell what kind of wine it is, he can."

"Luchresi cannot tell Amontillado from Sherry."

"And yet some say his taste in wine is as good as yours."

"Come, let us go."

"Where?"

"To your wine cellar."

"My friend, no; I can't impose on you like that. You're busy. Luchresi—"

"I'm not busy. Come."

"No, my friend, no. It's not just that. You have a cold, I see. My wine cellar is so damp. The walls are covered with mildew."

"Let us go, nevertheless. This cold is noth–ing. Amontillado! You have been cheated. And as for Luchresi, he can't tell Sherry from Amontillado."

As he spoke, Fortunato took my arm and put on his mask and cape. I let him hurry me to my villa.

There were no servants at home; they had run off to enjoy Carnival. I told them I wouldn't be home until morning. I ordered them not to stir from the house. That, I knew, would insure their immediate disappearance as soon as my back was turned.

I took down two torches and gave one to Fortunato. I reminded him to be careful as we descended. My wine cellar is inside the ancient underground burial chambers of my family, the catacombs of the Montresors.

My friend walked unsteadily. The bells on his cap jingled as he stumbled along.

"The cask," he said.

"It is farther on," I said. "Take a look at these walls."

He turned towards me, staring with drunken eyes.

"Mildew?" he asked.

"Mildew," I replied. "How long have you had that cough?"

"Ugh! ugh! ugh!—ugh! ugh! ugh!—ugh! ugh! ugh!"

My poor friend found it impossible to reply.

"It is nothing," he said at last.

"Come!" I said, "Let's go back; your health is too important. You might get sick, and I cannot be responsible. Besides, there is Luchresi—"

"Enough," he said. "I will not die from a cough."

"True," I replied. "And, indeed, I didn't want to alarm you—but we should take proper precautions. A drink of this Medoc wine will warm us."

I knocked off the neck of a bottle, one of a whole row of bottles lying on mold nearby.

"Drink," I said, handing him the wine.

He raised it to his lips with a smirk. His bells jingled.

"I drink," he said, "to the dead sleeping around us."

"And I drink to your long life."

He took my arm again and we proceeded.

"These burial chambers," he said, "are large."

"The Montresors," I replied, "were once a great family."

"I forget. What is your family's coat of arms?"

"A huge human foot crushing a snake with its fangs embedded in the heel."

"And your family motto?"

"No one injures me and gets away with it."

"Good!" he said.

The wine sparkled in his eyes and the bells jingled. We passed wall after wall of piled skeletons, with casks of wine here and there.

Entering the inmost part of the catacombs, I paused again. This time, I boldly took Fortunato by the arm.

"The mildew!" I said. "It hangs like moss on the walls. Drops of moisture trickle among the bones. Come! Let's go back before it's too late. Your cough—"

"Is nothing," he said. "Let us go on. But first, another sip of the Medoc."

I broke open another bottle. He emptied it. He laughed and threw the bottle upwards with a gesture I did not understand.

I looked at him in surprise. He repeated the gesture—a strange one.

"You do not understand?" he said. "You are not a Mason?"

"Yes, yes," I said. "Yes, yes."

"You? A Mason? Show me a sign."

"Here," I answered, bringing out a mason's trowel from the folds of my cape."*

"You must be joking," he cried out, shrinking back. "But let us go to the Amontillado."

"Fine," I said, putting the tool beneath my cloak and again offering him my arm. He leaned on it heavily. We passed through some low arches and, heading down, arrived at a deep crypt.

*Fortunato is referring to the Masons, an organization with many secret traditions. But the narrator has another kind of mason in mind when he pulls out a trowel, which is the tool of a stone mason's trade."

The air was so foul our torches barely glowed.

At the far end, we could see another, smaller crypt. Its walls were lined with human remains on three sides. On the fourth side, the bones had been thrown down on the ground in a large pile. With the bones removed, we could see yet one more crypt behind it about four feet deep. It was perhaps three feet wide and six or seven feet tall. It seemed to have been built for no particular use. It was just an empty space between two pillars, a niche. Behind it was the wall.

Fortunato, lifting his torch, tried to peer into the niche.

"Here," I said, "is the Amontillado. As for Luchresi—"

"He is an idiot," interrupted my friend, stepping forward unsteadily. I followed. When he reached the end of the niche, he staggered into the wall. He just stood there, dazed. In an instant, I had him in chains. In the rock wall two feet apart were two iron hooks. From one hung a short chain, from the other a padlock. Throwing the chain about Fortunato's waist, I had him secure in seconds. He was too amazed to resist. Taking the key from the lock, I stepped back.

"Pass your hand," I said, "over the wall. Feel the mildew. It is very damp. Once more I beg you to return. No? Then I must leave. But first, I must take good care of you."

"The Amontillado!" my friend cried out, still astonished.

"True," I replied, "the Amontillado."

As I said these words, I was digging into the pile of bones I mentioned before. I soon uncovered a supply of building stone and mortar. With my trowel, I began to wall up the entrance to the niche.

By the time I had laid the first tier of brick, Fortunato had sobered up quite a bit. The low moaning cry I heard was not the cry of a drunken man. Then there was a long silence. I laid the second tier, the third, and the fourth. Then I heard the chain shaking furiously. The noise lasted for several minutes. For greater satisfaction as I listened, I took a break and sat down on the bones. When the clanking quieted down, I quickly finished the fifth, sixth, and seventh tiers. The wall was now nearly as high as my chest. I paused. Holding up the torch, I threw a few feeble rays of light on the figure within.

Loud, shrill screams burst from the throat of the chained form. For a moment I hesitated. I trembled and moved back. Taking out my sword, I began to grope around inside the niche. Only after I put my hand on the solid wall was I reassured. I approached again, answering the shouts I heard. I mimicked everything Fortunato said. I yelled louder and stronger than he could. In a moment, he was quiet.

By midnight, the job was almost complete. I had finished the eighth, ninth and tenth tiers and a portion of the eleventh and final tier. I only needed to plaster in one last stone. I struggled with its weight. I placed it almost in position. Suddenly, from the niche came a low laugh that made the hairs on my head stand up. Then I heard a sad voice, which I hardly recognized as Fortunato's. The voice said—

"Ha! ha! ha!—he! he! he!—a very good joke, indeed—an excellent joke. We will have many a rich laugh about it at the villa—he! he! he!—over our wine—he! he! he!"

"The Amontillado!" I said.

"He! he! he!—he! he! he!—yes, the Amontillado. But is it not getting late? Everyone will be waiting for us. Let us be gone."

"Yes," I said, "let us be gone."

"For the love of God, Montresor!"

"Yes," I said, "for the love of God!"

I listened in vain for a reply. I grew impatient. I called aloud—

"Fortunato!"

No answer. I called again—

"Fortunato!"

No answer still. I pushed my torch through the only remaining space in the wall and let it fall inside. In return, I heard only a jingling of bells. My heart grew sick; it was the dampness of the burial chamber. I quickly finished my work. I forced the last stone into position and plastered it. Against the new wall, I re-assembled the old pile of bones. For fifty years no one has disturbed them.

Fortunato, rest in peace!

PREVIEW

More than 150 years after his death, Edgar Allan Poe is still one of the world's best-known writers of short horror stories. In "The Tell-Tale Heart," it's easy to see why. As the narrator explains the murder he has committed, Poe draws you deeper and deeper into the twisted depths of an insane mind.

THE TELL-TALE HEART

Edgar Allan Poe

It's true—I have been and am very, very, nervous! By why do you say that I'm insane? My senses are very sharp, not destroyed or dull. Most of all, my sense of hearing is very strong and sensitive. I have heard all things on earth, in heaven, and in hell. So how can you call me crazy? Listen and watch how sanely and calmly I tell you the whole story.

It is impossible to say how I first got the

idea, but once I thought of it, it haunted me day and night. I had nothing to gain and no anger as my motive. I loved the old man. He had never insulted me or done me any wrong. I didn't want his money. I think it was his eye; yes, that was it! He had the eye of a vulture—a pale blue eye with a film over it. Whenever he looked at me with that eye, my blood ran cold. So eventually I decided to kill the old man and get rid of that eye forever.

Now here is my point. You think I am insane. But madmen are idiots, and you should have seen *me*. You should have seen how smart and cautious I was; how clever and sneaky my plans were! The week before I killed the old man I was so nice to his face. But every night at midnight I opened his bedroom door gently. I stuck in my head and a dark lantern, which was closed so no light escaped. You would have laughed to see how smart I was when I did this! I moved very, very slowly, so I wouldn't wake up the old man. It took me an hour to move my whole head into the door opening so that I could see the old man sleeping on his bed. Ha! Would a madman have been that smart?

When my head was in the room, I carefully opened the lantern without creaking its hinges. I opened the lantern door enough that one thin ray of light shone on the old man's vulture eye. Although I did this at midnight every night for a week, his eyes were always closed. I couldn't bring myself to kill him with his eyes closed, because it wasn't the old man that bothered me, it was his evil eye. Each morning, I would walk boldly right into his room and speak to him nicely, asking him how he had slept. He would have had to have been very smart to suspect that every night at midnight I watched him while he slept.

On the eighth night, I was extra-careful opening the bedroom door. The minute hand of a watch moves more quickly than my hands did. That night I felt how powerful and clever I was. I could hardly hold in my feeling of victory. To think that there I was, opening the old man's door, and he had no idea of my secret plans. I almost laughed at the idea, and maybe he heard me, because he moved in his bed suddenly, like he was scared. You may think that I pulled back—but no. His room was pitch black since his shades and curtains were closed, so I knew he couldn't see me opening the door. I kept pushing it open, slowly but surely.

I had my head in, and was about to open the lantern when my thumb slipped. The old man sat up quickly in bed, shouting "Who's there?!"

I didn't move and said nothing. For an hour I didn't move a muscle, and he did not lie back down. I had listened to him for many nights, and now he was listening, hearing the warning of his own death.

After a while, I heard a small groan, and I knew it was the groan of total terror. It was not a groan of pain or sadness—oh no!—it was the deep sound that comes from the bottom of a soul full of fear. I knew that sound very well. Many nights at midnight I had felt that sound rising up inside of me, echoing my personal terrors. Although I knew what the old man felt, and felt sorry for him, I still laughed to myself. I knew he had been lying awake since he first sensed something in the room, with his fear growing all the time. He had been trying to reassure himself, saying, "It is only the wind— or a mouse—or a cricket." But he had not succeeded in comforting himself, because he felt Death stalking and overpowering him. Even though he didn't actually see or hear me, he sensed I was in the room because he felt that shadow of Death.

After patiently waiting for a long time, I decided to open the lantern a little. I carefully opened it and let out a small ray of light. The thread of light fell right upon the vulture eye! It was wide open, and I became furious when I saw it. I saw it clearly: a dull blue, with that hideous film over it that chilled me to the bone. I could see only his eye, because I had managed to direct the ray of light onto the eye alone.

Didn't I tell you before that what you think is insanity is actually just overly-sharp senses? At that moment I heard a low, dull, quick sound, like a watch ticking inside cotton. I knew what the sound was. It was the beating of the old man's heart. Hearing it made me even more angry.

But still I didn't move. I hardly breathed. I held the lantern completely still, seeing how steadily I could keep the light shining on that eye. The whole time the hellish beat of the old man's heart increased. Every minute it got faster and faster and louder and louder. The old man must have been extremely terrified! It grew louder, I tell you—louder every minute! Do you understand me? I have told you I am nervous; it's true. In the middle of the night in that silent old house, the strange noise of the heartbeat filled me with terror. For a few more minutes I kept still, but the beating grew louder and louder! I thought his old heart would burst! And now I felt a new fear; a neighbor would hear the loud heartbeat! The old man's time had come!

With a loud yell, I opened up the lantern completely and jumped into the room. The old man screamed once; only once. Instantly I dragged him to the floor and pulled his mattress on top of him. I smiled to see that my deed was almost done. However, for many minutes his heart continued to beat with a muffled sound. I didn't worry about this; no one would hear it through the wall. Finally it stopped. The old man was dead. I pulled off the mattress and examined the corpse. Yes, he was stone dead. I put my hand over his heart for many minutes, but there was no beat. He was dead, and his eye would bother me no more.

If you still think I'm crazy, you won't when I describe how carefully I hid the evidence of my crime. As morning approached, I worked quickly and silently. First of all, I cut up the body; I cut off the head, the arms and the legs. Then I pulled up three boards from the bedroom floor and hid the body under them. I put the boards back so cleverly and neatly that no human eye—not even *his*—could have seen that anything was wrong. There were no blood stains to wash out. I had been too careful for that—ha ha!

When I had finished working, it was 4 AM, and still as dark as midnight. As the clock struck four, I heard a knock at the front door. I went to open it with a light heart; for what was I afraid of now? Three police officers came in. They told me that a neighbor had heard a scream and had called the police, and they had a search warrant for the house.

I smiled; what did I have to be afraid of? I welcomed the policemen in and told them that I had a nightmare and it was I who had screamed. I mentioned that the old man was away in the country. I took them all over the house and asked them to search well. After a while, I took them to *his* bedroom. I showed them his belongings, all neat and in the right place. I was feeling so cocky that I asked them to sit down and rest in that room. I was so confident that I had committed the perfect crime that I put my own chair right over the spot where I had hidden the body.

The officers were satisfied. My relaxed attitude and mood had convinced them. We chatted and I cheerfully answered questions. However, after a while I started to wish they would leave. I had a headache, and I heard ringing in my ears, but they kept sitting and talking. As the ringing grew louder, I tried to talk more to distract me from the sound. Finally, I realized that the noise was *not* coming from inside my ears.

My face must have gotten very pale, but I kept talking faster and louder. Still, the sound increased, and what could I do? What I heard was *a low, dull, quick sound, like a watch ticking inside cotton*! I gasped, but the policemen didn't seem to hear it. The more I talked, the more the sound increased. Why didn't they leave? I paced the floor as we talked, but still, it got louder! Oh God! What could I do? I started swearing and yelling and foaming at the mouth! I lifted the chair and crashed it to the floor, but it didn't hide the sound, which grew louder—louder—louder! Still, the policemen talked pleasantly, and smiled. Was it *possible* they didn't hear it? Oh no! They heard! They suspected! They *knew*! I felt they were making fun of my horror. Anything was better than this torture! I could no longer bear their false smiles. I thought I would either scream, or die. There it was again! Listen to it: louder, louder, louder, *louder*!

"You monsters!" I screamed. "Stop pretending! I admit to the murder! Look here, and tear up the floor! It is the beating of his hideous heart!"

PREVIEW

The local schoolmaster, Ichabod Crane, is an ambitious man. He wants to marry the rich and beautiful Katrina Van Tassel. To win her heart, the clownish teacher will have to win out over his muscular and handsome rival, Brom Bones. He will also have to conquer his own overactive imagination and, perhaps, the legendary Headless Horseman of Sleepy Hollow.

THE LEGEND OF SLEEPY HOLLOW

Washington Irving

On the eastern shore of the Hudson River lies Tarry Town. How did the little village get such a name? Some people say wives from nearby towns accused their shiftless husbands of tarrying there, wasting time doing nothing. I do not know if that is true. I relate such information only to assure the reader my report is complete and accurate.

Two miles from Tarry Town is a valley, one

of the quietest places in the whole world. The babbling of the small brook there is barely loud enough to lull you to sleep. Only the tapping of a woodpecker interrupts the silence.

As a child, I wandered into that valley the first time I tried to hunt. I shot at a squirrel in a grove of tall walnut trees. All I managed to do was scare myself, startled by the roar of a gun in such a peaceful place.

If you ever want to run away from the world, I know of no better spot than that peaceful valley. Because of the lazy calm of the place and its people, it has long been known as Sleepy Hollow. And rightly so. A drowsy dreaminess hangs over the land. Some say a German doctor had bewitched the place. Others say it was an old Indian chief. But it is certain that some kind of spell haunts the good people who live there. They sleepwalk through their days. They see visions. They hear music and voices in the air. Strange tales, ghostly haunts, and superstitions fill the whole neighborhood. More shooting stars flash across Sleepy Hollow than anywhere else in the country. More nightmares visit sleepers there, too.

One phantom above all others haunts this enchanted zone, an eerie man with no head. He always appears on horseback. He commands all of the spirits. Some say he died in the American Revolution, his head carried away by a cannonball. Now he rides, in the valley and beyond. He returns time and again to a church not very far away. Buried there—historians agree—is the body of a mounted soldier, a cavalryman who fought with the British. Every night, the ghost rides out in search of his head. That cold blast of wind you feel there just before daybreak? That is the horseman galloping back to the churchyard, racing the sun.

So the legend claims. Many wild stories have sprung up about this terrible ghost. Most every night, tales are told around country firesides about the Headless Horseman of Sleepy Hollow.

Anyone who visits—even for a short time— soaks up the spirit of the valley. You may enter wide-awake. But you leave imagining things, dreaming dreams, and seeing ghosts.

While America keeps changing all around it, this peaceful spot stays the same. Many years have passed since I last visited Sleepy Hollow. But if I went there today, I'm sure I could still find the same trees and the same families loafing underneath their shade.

Let me take you back now to a distant period of American history—some thirty years ago. In that out of the way corner of the natural and supernatural world lived a worthy gentleman. He tarried in Sleepy Hollow to teach the children who lived there. This schoolmaster,

Ichabod Crane, was well named. He looked very much like a crane. He was tall and extremely thin. He had narrow shoulders, long arms and legs, hands that dangled a mile out of his sleeves, and feet like shovels. His head was small and flat on top. Everything about him hung together, but only loosely. His huge ears, large green glassy eyes, and long beak-like nose made his head look like the rooster on an old-fashioned weather vane. No doubt, his enormous snout did catch enough breeze to point his scrawny head in the direction of the wind. Striding along on a gusty day with his clothes fluttering, he looked like a scarecrow escaped from the cornfield.

The schoolhouse was one large room, crudely constructed of logs. Some of its windows had glass. Others were nothing more than openings patched with papers from old copybooks. It stood at the foot of a woody hill, with a brook running close by, and a large birch tree growing at one end. From there you could hear the low murmur of pupils' voices, like the hum of a beehive. Now and then the teacher would holler. Now and then you could hear the terrible sound of the schoolmaster giving special encouragement to one troublemaker or another. Crane firmly believed, "Spare the rod and you will spoil the child." Ichabod's scholars were not spoiled.

Now, I don't want you to think he was a cruel man. He took no pleasure in such tasks. He administered justice carefully. He passed by the frail fellows terrified at the sight of the birch rod. But the tough, wrong-headed lads got a double dose. This he called "doing his duty by their parents." After inflicting punishment, he always promised the sore brat "he would remember it and thank him for it."

When school hours were over, the master was even the companion and playmate of the larger boys. On holiday afternoons he would take some of the smaller ones home. He was especially interested in those students who happened to have pretty older sisters or mothers known for their cooking. Indeed, it paid Ichabod to keep on good terms with his pupils. A teacher's salary was small indeed. It barely paid enough to keep him fed. Though thin, he had the appetite of an anaconda. To make-up for the low salary, it was the custom in that country for the teacher to live at the houses of the farmers whose children he taught. There he slept and ate for free. So Ichabod lived a week at a time with each set of parents. Once every seven days or so, he could be seen moving to the next farm with everything he owned tied up in a large cotton handkerchief.

To make sure he was not a burden to his hosts, Ichabod made himself useful and pleasant.

Sometimes, he assisted the farmers in the lighter farm work. He helped make hay, mended the fences, took the horses to water, drove the cows from pasture, and cut wood for the winter fire. He also softened his personality. As a guest, he did not act at all like the disciplinarian ruling over his pupils. Instead, he became gentle, constantly flattering those on whom he depended. He found favor in the eyes of the mothers by caring for the children, particularly the youngest. He would sit with a child on one knee, while rocking a cradle with his foot for hours.

In addition to his other jobs, Ichabod taught young folks the singing of psalms. This meant more to the schoolmaster than the extra money he earned. Every Sunday, Ichabod proudly sang in church with the choir. He believed more attention came his way than to the preacher. Certainly, his voice was louder than any other in the congregation. The peculiar high-pitched sounds you can still hear today in the church—and a half a mile away beside the millpond—first came from Ichabod's nose.

So, with a series of odd jobs, the schoolmaster got by. The folks of the community—who did not understand the difficulty of teaching—thought he had it easy.

The females in many rural communities consider the schoolmaster an important person.

He is thought to be a gentleman of superior style and learning. A visit from the local teacher, therefore, is apt to mean the serving of special food. Thanks to the cakes and other treats he was bound to get, Ichabod greatly enjoyed the company of ladies. At every opportunity, you would find him among them. He would entertain the country women between services on Sunday by gathering wild grapes and reciting the lines on the gravestones in the churchyard.

As a result of his travels, Ichabod knew and spread around all the local gossip. This added to his appeal. In addition, he was regarded as a man of great learning. He had read several books from beginning to end. He knew almost by heart Cotton Mather's *History of New England Witchcraft*. And he believed every word.

Ichabod Crane was an odd mixture of cleverness and simplemindedness. He had always believed in the supernatural. His interest had grown as a result of his stay in Sleepy Hollow. No tale was too monstrous for him to swallow. Many days, he would read over Mather's frightening tales of witches and the devil from the end of school until darkness. Then he would have to make his way home. He would pass swamp and stream and terrifying woodland. His imagination magnified every sound of nature—the moan of the whippoorwill, the cry of the tree toad, the dreary hooting of the screech owl. Even fireflies startled him. If a beetle accidentally flew into him, the poor chap was ready to faint dead away. Only the singing of psalms could calm him. The citizens of Sleepy Hollow were astonished whenever they heard that haunting nasal melody floating along some twilight road.

Another of Ichabod's guilty pleasures was spending long winter evenings with aged farmwives as they sat by the fire. He would listen to their marvelous tales of ghosts and goblins, and haunted fields, and haunted brooks, and haunted bridges, and haunted houses, and particularly of the Headless Horseman. In turn, he would delight the old women with stories of witchcraft. He would scare them with theories about comets and shooting stars. Most frightening of all was the alarming fact that the world turned, and they were upside down half the time!

All this was pleasant enough by the comfort of a crackling fire. But Ichabod paid for his pleasure on the walk home. What fearful shapes and shadows crossed his path! Every ray of light streaming from some distant window made him tremble! How often was he horrified by a ghostly figure that turned out to be a bush covered with snow! How often did his blood curdle at the sound of his own footsteps on the crusted snow! He dared not look over his shoulder, afraid some beast was following close behind. How often he panicked at a gust of wind, sure it was the Headless Horseman himself!

Yet he knew somehow that these phantoms were all in his mind. Daylight put an end to all such evils. So Ichabod could have had a comfortable life despite the Devil and all his works. Then, however, he encountered the being that causes more trouble for men than all the ghosts, goblins, and witches put together. He met... a woman.

One of his music pupils was Katrina Van Tassel, the only child of a well-off Dutch farmer. She was a fresh-faced girl of eighteen, shapely and rosy-cheeked. She was famous throughout the valley for her beauty and her ambition. A flirtatious woman, she wore golden jewelry and a petticoat short enough to display the prettiest foot and ankle in the vicinity.

Ichabod Crane had a soft spot for women and a foolish heart. It is no surprise that his wandering eyes fell on a morsel as tempting as Katrina, especially after he visited her father's mansion. Old Baltus Van Tassel was a thriving, openhearted farmer. He had seldom ventured beyond the old homestead. There, everything was snug, happy, and familiar. He was satisfied with his wealth, but not too proud.

Van Tassel's country manor on the banks of the Hudson was hidden away. Over it, a great elm tree spread its broad branches. A spring of the softest and sweetest water bubbled up nearby. Its water sparkled away into a brook babbling along among the willows. Close by the farmhouse was a barn as large as a church. It was filled to bursting with farm treasures. Fat pigs grunted in their pens. Now and then, piglets trooped out. Snowy geese floated in a nearby pond. Regiments of turkeys gobbled through the farmyard. Before the barn door strutted the gallant rooster, tearing up the earth with his feet. Every so often he called his ever-hungry family to enjoy some tidbit he'd uncovered.

The schoolmaster's mouth watered as he gazed upon the farm's promise of delicious food all winter long. He pictured to himself every roasting-pig running about with a pudding in his belly and an apple in his mouth. He imagined the ducks paired together cozily in dishes with onion sauce. In every porker, he saw a sleek side of bacon and some juicy ham.

Ichabod filled with delight at the sight of the abundant fields surrounding the Van Tassel home. His heart yearned for Katrina, the fair damsel who would one day inherit this wealth. In his imagination he was already using his newfound riches to buy land and mansions in the frontier. He saw himself with Katrina and a whole family of children setting out for Kentucky, Tennessee—or Lord knows where!

The moment Ichabod crossed the step of the Van Tassel residence, the conquest of his heart was complete. It was one of those roomy farmhouses built in the style of the first Dutch settlers. Its low projecting roof formed a covered entrance along the front. Under this were hung harnesses and nets for fishing in the neighboring river. Benches were built along the sides for summer use. A great spinning wheel stood at one end. A butter churn at the other end showed the many uses of this porch.

Ichabod entered the hall at the center of the mansion. Here, rows of pitchers, bowls, and candlesticks dazzled his eyes. In one corner stood a huge bag of wool, ready to be spun. Ears of Indian corn, red peppers, and strings of dried apples and peaches decorated the walls. Through an open door, he glimpsed the best parlor. Its claw-footed chairs and dark mahogany tables were polished to a mirror-like shine. The fireplace tongs and log frame glistened. Trinkets shaped like oranges and conch shells decorated the mantelpiece. Strings of various-colored birds' eggs hung above. A great ostrich egg was suspended in the center of the room. A corner cupboard, left open on purpose, displayed a treasure trove of old silver and well-mended china.

From this moment, Ichabod would not have peace of mind until he could gain the affections of Katrina Van Tassel. This task, however, would prove more difficult than the quests of knights of old. They only had to deal with giants, enchanters, and fiery dragons to win the hand of a lady. Ichabod, on the other hand, had to conquer the heart of a flirtatious country girl. And he had to best all of Katrina's many admirers. Each one tried every possible means to win her heart. Each one kept a watchful and angry eye on the other.

Among these suitors, the most formidable opponent was a muscular, roaring, country boy. His given name, Abraham, had long ago been shortened to Brom. The valley rang with stories of its local hero. Broad-shouldered, black haired, square jawed, and muscular, everyone called him BROM BONES. Everyone for miles around knew him. His skill on horseback was legendary. He won every race and contest of strength. Due to his superior powers, he served as the judge for all disputes. He pronounced his decisions with a tone that ruled out any appeal. He was always ready for a fight or a frolic. He was mischievous but not wicked. There was a strong dash of good humor in him.

Brom had three or four buddies who modeled themselves after him. Together they combed the countryside, out for fun. In cold weather, Brom wore a fur cap topped with a fox's tail. Anytime this hat was spied at any gathering, everyone expected trouble. Brom and his crew would gallop past farmhouses at midnight with a whoop and a holler. Old ladies, startled out of their sleep, would listen for a moment and then say, "Ay, there goes Brom Bones and his gang!" The neighbors looked upon him with a mixture of fear, admiration, and goodwill. Brom took the blame for every prank and brawl in the vicinity.

Brom, too, had singled out Katrina Van Tassel as the object of his affection. Though he was as subtle as a bear, rumor had it that Katrina did not completely discourage his hopes. When Brom's horse was seen outside Van Tassel's on a Sunday night, all other suitors rode right by.

Brom, then, was Ichabod Crane's chief rival. Any other man would have retired from the competition. Ichabod, however, was like a willow branch; though he bent, he never broke. And, though he bent under the slightest pressure, the moment it was gone he was ready again.

Ichabod knew he could not defeat this rival in open battle. So he courted Katrina gently and quietly. As Katrina's singing teacher, Ichabod had an excuse to visit frequently. He had nothing to fear from Katrina's parents—often a stumbling block in the path of lovers. Balt Van Tassel loved his daughter better even than his pipe. A reasonable man and an excellent father, he let her have her way in everything. His wife had enough to do to take care of her household. As she said, "Ducks and geese are foolish things and must be looked after, but girls can take care of themselves." She bustled about the house. Balt sat smoking his evening pipe. In the meanwhile, Ichabod courted their daughter by the side of the spring under the great elm.

I admit to knowing nothing about how women's hearts are won. To me they are a riddle. Some seem to have only one weakness. Others may be captured in a thousand different ways. He who wins a hundred ordinary hearts deserves some recognition. But he who keeps undisputed control over the heart of a flirt is a hero. Even the mighty Brom Bones could not claim such a victory. In fact, from the moment Ichabod Crane came calling, Brom's interest seemed to fade. His horse was no longer seen tied outside on Sunday nights. Gradually, a deadly feud arose between Brom Bones and the schoolmaster.

Brom preferred open warfare. He would have chosen to battle for the hand of the fair Katrina man-to-man. Ichabod was well aware of the superior might of his foe. He had even overheard Bones boast that he would "fold the schoolmaster in two and lay him on a shelf in his own schoolhouse." Instead, Brom turned to his mischievous side. He began playing rude practical jokes on his rival. Bones and his gang persecuted Ichabod without mercy. They disturbed his peace, smoked out his singing-school by stopping up the chimney, broke into the schoolhouse at night and turned everything topsy-turvy. The superstitious schoolmaster began to think all the witches in the country held meetings there. Still more annoying, Brom made fun of Ichabod in front of his beloved. He even taught his dog to whine on command, claiming the dog was better suited to teach singing than Ichabod.

So matters went on for some time. There was no change in the standing of the rivals. One fine fall afternoon, Ichabod sat, deep in thought, keeping an eye on his students. In his hand he held a ruler, the symbol of his power. On the wall behind him hung the birch rod of justice. On his desk he piled everything he'd confiscated from the students: half-munched apples, popguns, and enough paper cannonballs to supply a division. Someone must have been punished moments before, because every student was busily intent upon his books or slyly whispering with one eye on the master. The stillness was suddenly interrupted by the appearance of a servant mounted on the back of a ragged colt. He came clattering up to the school door with an invitation for Ichabod to attend a party to be held that evening at Mr. Van Tassel's.

Suddenly the schoolroom became a beehive

of activity. The pupils were hurried through their lessons. The clever students simply skipped over half and got away with it. A quick application of encouragement to the rear of those who worked slowly made them toil more quickly. Books were thrown aside without being put away on the shelves, inkstands were overturned, benches were thrown down, and everyone was dismissed an hour early.

The valiant Ichabod spent an extra half hour trying to make himself presentable. To arrive in style, the schoolmaster borrowed a horse from his host of the week. Thus gallantly mounted, he rode forth in a quest for adventure. It is only fitting I should, in the true spirit of romance, describe our hero and his noble steed. The animal he rode was a broken-down plow-horse that had outlived its usefulness but not its viciousness. He was bony and shaggy. His rusty mane and tail were tangled and knotted with burrs. One of his eyes had no pupil; the empty socket glared in a ghostly way. His good eye gleamed devilishly. He must have been a fiery colt judging from his name, Gunpowder. He had been, at one time, the favorite mount of his master, a furious rider and a very irritable man. Some of the master's spirit must have found its way into the animal. Old and broken-down as he looked, he had more of the lurking devil in him than any wild stallion.

Ichabod suited his horse perfectly. He rode with short stirrups, which brought his knees nearly up to the top of the saddle. His sharp elbows stuck out like a grasshopper's. As his horse trotted on, the motion of his arms was not unlike the flapping of a pair of wings. A small wool hat rested almost on the top of his nose. The tails of his black coat fluttered out almost to the horse's tail. A phantom as strange looking as Ichabod is rarely seen in broad daylight.

It was a fine fall day. The forests were mostly brown and yellow, though frost had colored some trees with brilliant dyes of orange, purple, and scarlet. From time to time, streaming files of wild geese were seen flying south.

As Ichabod rode slowly on his way, his eye, as always, spotted all the food this abundant autumn offered. He noticed every apple. Some hung on trees. Some had already been gathered in baskets for the market. Others, heaped up in piles, awaited the cider press. Farther on, he observed great fields of corn and imagined cakes and puddings. Pumpkins offered the promise of delicious pies. Seeing fields of buckwheat, Ichabod imagined stacks of pancakes swimming in butter and honey, served by the delicate little hand of Katrina Van Tassel.

Toward evening, Ichabod arrived at the Van Tassel place. It was crowded with guests. Old farmers with leathery faces in homemade coats, blue stockings, and huge shoes with magnificent pewter buckles. Their shrunken little wives, in modest caps and long-waisted dresses with calico pockets. Full-bodied lasses with clothes as old-fashioned as their mothers' except for the addition of a straw hat or a fine ribbon just like the girls in the city. Sons with their long locks tied back, especially if they could come up with an eel skin, thought to strengthen the hair.

Brom Bones was, as usual, the center of attention. He rode to the gathering on Daredevil, a horse that—like him—was full of mischief. No one but Brom could manage the beast. Brom had always preferred vicious animals. He considered a tame horse unworthy for a spirited lad.

When Ichabod entered the mansion he could see one thing only. Not the crowds of lovely young ladies. He gazed, spellbound, at a sumptuous banquet. Heaped up platters of doughnuts, sweet cakes and short cakes, ginger cakes and honey cakes, the whole family of cakes. Pies: apple, peach, and pumpkin. Slices of ham and smoked beef and delectable dishes of preserved plums, peaches, and pears. Broiled shad and roasted chickens together with bowls of milk and cream, rather randomly set out on tables.

I wish I could give this banquet the time it deserves, but I am eager to get on with my story. However, Ichabod Crane was not in such a hurry. He managed to sample every treat.

Ichabod's spirits rose as his stomach filled. He ate, chuckling to himself that one day he might be lord of all this luxury and splendor. He'd turn his back on the old schoolhouse. He'd snap his fingers in the face of everyone who ever disrespected him.

Old Baltus Van Tassel moved among his company with a face as round and jolly as the harvest moon. He shook hands, slapped backs, laughed out loud, and told his guests to "help themselves."

And now the sound of the music called everyone to the dance. The musician was an old fiddler, the traveling orchestra of the neighborhood for fifty years.

Ichabod prided himself on his dancing as much as his singing. When he danced, every part of him was in full motion. What else could you expect from the spanker of rascals? He was full of energy and joy. Katrina, the lady of his heart, was his partner. She smiled politely at his flirtations. In the meanwhile, Brom Bones sat by himself in one corner, brooding.

When the dance ended, Ichabod joined a group of older folks gossiping and telling exaggerated stories of their exploits in the American Revolution. Sleepy Hollow had been near enough to the front lines to see some raids and a few refugees. Enough time had passed since the war for each storyteller to become the hero of every adventure.

Doffue Martling would have captured a British ship with his rifle if it hadn't broken apart on the sixth shot. And there was an old gentleman who stopped a musket-ball with his sword. He was ready anytime to show the slightly bent blade. There were several more equally great heroes. Each one felt personally responsible for the American victory.

But, even these yarns could not compare to the ghost stories that followed. Superstitions thrive in out-of-the-way places like Sleepy Hollow. Where people come and go such stories get lost. We seldom hear of ghosts except in established communities. But, in this case, the spirit of Sleepy Hollow itself added to the number of supernatural legends. Several Sleepy Hollow people were present at Van Tassel's, and were spinning wild and wonderful yarns. They told about the mournful cries heard near the great tree where Major Andre, the British spy, was captured. They told of the woman in white, who haunted the dark glen at Raven Rock, and was often heard to shriek on winter nights. She had died there in a snowstorm. Most of the stories, however, involved the favorite specter of Sleepy Hollow, the Headless Horseman. He had been heard several times recently, patrolling nearby. It was said he tied his horse up every night among the graves in the churchyard.

The remote location of this church made it a favorite haunt of troubled spirits. It stands on a hill, surrounded by locust trees and elms. Looking at its grassy yard, one might think the dead could rest in peace there. On one side of the church extends a forest and a large brook roaring among broken rocks and trunks of fallen trees. Over a deep black part of the stream, not far from the church, is a wooden bridge. The road leading to it and the bridge itself are thickly shaded by trees. A gloom covers the area, even in the daytime. At night it is even more fearful. Here is the favorite haunt of the Headless Horseman, the place where he is most frequently found. Old Brouwer told how he met the Horseman one night returning from Sleepy Hollow. Together, they'd galloped over hill and swamp until they reached the bridge. Suddenly, the Horseman turned into a skeleton and threw old Brouwer into the brook. Then he sprang away over the treetops with a clap of thunder.

This story was immediately matched by an adventure of Brom Bones three times more marvelous. To him, the headless cavalryman was little more than a second-rate horseman. Returning one night from the neighboring village, Brom began, he had been overtaken by this midnight rider. Brom challenged him to a race. Before long, Daredevil was beating the goblin horse by more than a length. As they came to the church bridge, the soldier made a run for it and vanished in a flash of fire.

Every tale sank deep in the mind of Ichabod. He responded with passages from his favorite author, Cotton Mather. Then he added legends from his home state, Connecticut. He finished by recounting the fearful sights he had seen in his nightly walks around Sleepy Hollow.

The party gradually broke up. The old farmers gathered together their families. Their wagons could be heard for some time rattling along the rocky roads and distant hills. Some young women left mounted behind their favorite admirer. Their lighthearted laughter echoed along the silent woodlands. The hoof beats of their horses sounded fainter and fainter until they gradually died away. The house grew silent and deserted.

Ichabod stayed behind to have a moment alone with Katrina, the woman of his dreams. He was convinced he was now on the high road to success. What happened at this interview I cannot pretend to say, for in fact I do not know. Something, however, must have gone wrong. Ichabod departed a short while later quite grim-faced and miserable. Was he the victim of a flirt's tricks? Had she encouraged him just to make his rival jealous? Heaven only knows! Ichabod seemed more like someone who had stolen a hen than a fair lady's heart. Without even glancing at the Van Tassel treasures, he went straight to the stable. He roughly awakened his nag from a sound sleep. The horse had been dreaming of mountains of oats and valleys of clover.

At the very witching time of night Ichabod headed home with a heavy heart. The hour was as bleak as he was. In the dead hush of midnight, he could even hear the barking of a watchdog from the opposite shore of the Hudson. Now and then a rooster would crow, sounding dream-like. Ichabod saw no signs of life. He heard only the unhappy chirp of the cricket or the twang of a bullfrog from a nearby pond.

The schoolmaster began to recall the stories of ghosts and goblins he had heard that day. The night grew darker and darker. The stars sank deeper in the sky, sometimes hidden by clouds. He had never felt so lonely and miser-able. Now, he was approaching the very place where many of the ghost stories had been set. In the center of the road stood an enormous poplar, towering like a giant above all the other trees. Its limbs were twisted and enormous, each one large enough to be the trunk of an ordinary tree. Near it, the unfortunate Andre had been taken prison-er. The tree was widely known as Major Andre's Tree. The common people regarded it with a mixture of respect and superstition. They felt sorry for the major to be sure. But there were also by now so many other tales of strange sights in the area.

As Ichabod approached this fearful tree, he began to whistle. His whistle was answered. No, it was just a gust of wind blowing through the dry branches. He got closer. He paused and stopped whistling. Something white was hanging from the trunk. No, it was just a place where the tree had been hit by lightning and the bark removed. He heard a groan. His teeth chattered and his knees banged against the saddle. It was just the rubbing of one huge branch against another in the breeze. He passed the tree in safety, but new perils lay before him.

About two hundred yards from the tree, a small brook crossed the road. From there, it ran into Wiley's Swamp. A few rough logs, laid side by side, served for a bridge over the stream. Where the brook entered the wood, a group of oaks and chestnuts—matted thick with wild grapevines—threw a deep gloom over the road. To pass this bridge was the most difficult trial. At this very spot, Andre was captured. Since then, the stream has been considered haunted. Every schoolboy who has to pass it alone after dark is fearful indeed.

As Ichabod approached the stream, his heart began to thump. He calmed his nerves, gave his horse a kick in the ribs, and attempted a dash across the bridge. The ornery old animal only moved sideways, bumping up against the fence. Ichabod, more scared than ever, jerked the reins and gave Gunpowder a kick. The horse started up all right, but only to plunge into a thicket of thorns on the opposite side of the road. The schoolmaster now used his whip and his heels. Old Gunpowder tore ahead, snuffling and snorting, but stopped right before the bridge. So suddenly had he halted that he nearly sent Ichabod sprawling. Just at this moment a splash by the side of the bridge caught the sensitive ear of Ichabod. In the dark shadow of the grove, on the edge of the brook, he saw something huge, deformed, and towering. It did not move. It seemed gathered up in the gloom, a gigantic monster ready to spring upon the traveler.

The schoolmaster's hair stood up on end. What could he do? It was too late to turn and fly away. What chance was there anyway of outrunning a ghost or goblin? After all, they could ride on the wings of the wind. Summoning up, therefore, a show of courage, he stuttered, "Who are you?" No reply. He repeated his demand in a voice even more agitated. Still there was no answer. Once more he hit the sides of the rigid Gunpowder. Ichabod shut his eyes and began singing a psalm. Just then the shadowy form began to move. It scrambled up and, in an instant, stood in the middle of the road. Though the night was dismal, Ichabod could now make out the mysterious figure. He appeared to be a horseman of large dimensions on a powerful black horse. He attempted neither to injure nor greet the schoolmaster. Instead, he kept to one side of the road, jogging along on the blind side of Gunpowder, who had recovered from his fright.

Ichabod did not appreciate this strange midnight companion. Remembering the adventure of Brom Bones with the Headless Horseman, he hurried his horse along. The stranger, however, quickened his horse to the same speed. Ichabod slowed up, his horse walking now. He thought in this way he could lag behind. The ghostly figure did the same. Ichabod's heart began to sink. He tried singing again, but his parched tongue stuck to the roof of his mouth. He could not utter a note. The stubborn silence of his companion was terrible and mysterious, until it was soon explained... in a horrifying way. At the top of the hill, the schoolmaster could see the silhouette of his fellow traveler against the sky. Ichabod was horror-struck on realizing that he was headless! His horror increased when he saw that the head was carried before him on his saddle! The schoolmaster's terror rose to desperation. He rained a shower of kicks and blows on Gunpowder. The horse responded by charging ahead, but the ghost rider stayed step for step with him. Away they sped, stones flying and sparks flashing at every bound. Ichabod's flimsy outfit fluttered in the air as he stretched his long body over his horse's head.

They had now reached the turn off to Sleepy Hollow. Gunpowder, who seemed possessed, turned the other way and plunged recklessly downhill with the ghost horse close behind. This road leads through a low spot shaded by trees for about a quarter of a mile. Then it crosses the bridge famous in the goblin story. Just beyond, stands the white church and its graveyard.

Thanks to the panic of his old horse, Crane—though an unskillful rider—had been able to stay ahead. But when he was halfway through the shaded area, his saddle gave way and started slipping from under him. He tried to hold it, but in vain. He just had time to save himself by grabbing old Gunpowder around the neck. The saddle fell to the earth. He heard it trampled by his pursuer. For a moment he worried about the horse's owner. It was his Sunday saddle. But this was no time for petty fears. The goblin was close behind him. Ichabod had enough to do to stay in his seat. Sometimes he slipped to one side. Sometimes he slipped to the other. Sometimes he was thrown onto the high ridge of his horse's backbone. Crane feared another jolt would split him in half.

An opening in the trees gave the schoolmaster some hope. The church bridge was at hand. He saw the walls of the church dimly glaring under the trees beyond. He remembered the place where Brom Bones' ghostly competitor had disappeared. "If I can only reach that bridge," thought Ichabod, "I am safe." Just then he heard the black steed panting, close behind. He even thought he felt its hot breath. Another kick in the ribs and old Gunpowder sprang onto the bridge. His hooves thundered over the booming planks. In an instant, he had gained the opposite side. Ichabod cast a look behind, expecting to witness his pursuer vanish in a flash of fire. That's what was supposed to happen. Instead, he saw the goblin rising in his stirrups about to throw his head at the petrified schoolmaster. Ichabod tried to duck, but too late. It met his skull with a tremendous crash. He was thrown headfirst into the dust. Gunpowder, the goblin rider, and the black steed passed by like a whirlwind.

The next morning the old horse was found without his saddle. He was calmly grazing in the grass at his master's gate, the bridle under his feet. Ichabod did not show up at breakfast. Dinner-hour came, but no Ichabod. The boys assembled at the schoolhouse then played the whole day. No schoolmaster. Ichabod's host became uneasy about the fate of the poor fellow, and about his saddle. Some diligent investigating revealed traces of Ichabod. On the road leading to the church, the saddle was found, trampled in the dirt. Horse tracks had made deep dents in the road. Evidently, the rider had been traveling at a furious speed. The tracks were traced to the bridge. Beyond that, on the bank of the brook where the water ran deepest and darkest, they found Ichabod's hat. Close beside it was a shattered pumpkin.

The brook was searched, but no body was discovered. Ichabod's landlord examined the bundle containing everything the missing schoolmaster owned:

Two shirts and a half;

Two neck cloths;

One or two pair of woolen stockings;

One rusty razor;

One tattered book of psalm tunes.

The books and furniture of the schoolhouse belonged to the community, except for Cotton Mather's *History of Witchcraft*, an Almanac, and a book of dreams and fortunetelling. Scribbled on a sheet of paper were several unsuccessful attempts to copy a poem in honor of Katrina. Ichabod's last host quickly burned the magic books. He vowed never to send his children to school again. Whatever money the schoolmaster had possessed was gone. It must have been on him at the time of his disappearance.

At church the next Sunday, everyone talked about the mysterious event. The curious gathered in the churchyard, at the bridge, and at the spot where the hat and pumpkin had been found. People recalled the stories of Brouwer and of Bones. After comparing them to the evidence in this case, they came to the conclusion that Ichabod had been carried off by the Headless Horseman. As he was a bachelor, and didn't owe anyone any money, he was quickly forgotten. Eventually, the school was moved and a new teacher was hired.

Sometime later, an old farmer who had visited New York heard—on good authority—that Ichabod Crane was still alive. He had run off for fear of the goblin and his host as well as disappointment over his failure to woo Katrina. It was said Ichabod had moved to a distant part of the country. He taught school and studied law at the same time. He became a lawyer, a politician, and eventually, a judge.

Soon after the schoolmaster's disappearance, Brom Bones led Katrina in triumph to the altar. Folks noticed Brom seemed to have a knowing look on his face every time Ichabod was discussed. And, he couldn't help but laugh when anyone mentioned the pumpkin. Some people began to suspect he knew more than he chose to tell.

The old country wives, however, who are

the best judges of these matters, believe to this day that spirits carried Ichabod away. The tale of Ichabod Crane has become the favorite story to tell around an evening fire. The locals are more superstitious than ever about the bridge. That may explain why the road was modified. Now it approaches the church closer to the millpond. The deserted schoolhouse soon fell into ruin. It was said to be haunted by the ghost of the unfortunate schoolmaster. Farm boys making their way home on a summer evening still claim to hear Ichabod's voice in the distance, singing a sad psalm amid the silence of Sleepy Hollow.

PREVIEW

What a miserable fellow old Ebenezer Scrooge is! He almost seems to enjoy taking the happiness out of any occasion—even Christmas. But on one remarkable Christmas Eve, gloomy old Mr. Scrooge receives some surprise visitors. Who are these unexpected callers? They're not exactly friends . . . they're not exactly neighbors . . . in fact, they're not exactly alive...

A CHRISTMAS CAROL

Charles Dickens

CHAPTER 1
Marley's Ghost

Marley was dead. There is no doubt whatever about that. The record of his burial was signed by the clergyman, the clerk, the undertaker, and the chief mourner. Old Marley was as dead as a doornail.

Scrooge never painted out Old Marley's name. There it stood, years afterward, above the warehouse door: Scrooge and Marley.

He was tightfisted, was Scrooge! a squeezing, wrenching, grasping, scraping, clutching, miserly old sinner! Hard and sharp as flint and solitary as an oyster. His cold nature froze his old features, nipped his pointed nose, shriveled his cheek, stiffened his gait, made his eyes red and his thin lips blue. A frosty coating was on his head, and on his eyebrows, and his wiry chin. No wind that blew was bitterer than he.

Nobody ever stopped him in the street to say, "My dear Scrooge, how are you? When will you come to see me?" No beggars pleaded with him for coins. No children asked him what time it was. No man or woman ever asked him the way to any place. Even the blind men's dogs appeared to know him. When they saw him coming, they would tug their owners into dark doorways.

But what did Scrooge care? He preferred to keep his distance from all humankind.

One Christmas Eve old Scrooge sat busy in his counting house. It was cold, bleak, biting weather. The city clocks had just struck three in the afternoon, but it was quite dark already. The fog came pouring in at every chink and keyhole, and it was difficult to see the houses across the street.

The door of Scrooge's office was open so that he might keep his eye upon his clerk. This poor soul occupied a tiny office, much like a dismal cell. The clerk was occupied in copying letters. Scrooge had a very small fire, but the clerk's fire was so small that it looked like one coal. He couldn't replenish it, however, for Scrooge kept the coal-box in his own room and guarded it carefully. So the clerk put on his long coat and tried to warm himself by sitting close to the candle. It was no use.

"A merry Christmas, Uncle! God save you!" cried a cheerful voice. It was the voice of Scrooge's nephew, who suddenly appeared before the old man.

"Bah!" said Scrooge, "Humbug!"

Having walked rapidly through the fog and frost, Scrooge's nephew was all in a glow. His face was ruddy and handsome, and his eyes sparkled.

"Christmas a humbug, Uncle?" said

Scrooge's nephew. "You don't mean that, I am sure."

"I do," said Scrooge. "Merry Christmas! What right have you to be merry? What reason do you have to be merry? You're so poor."

"Come, then," returned the nephew gaily. "What right have you to be dismal? What reason do you have to be sad? You're so rich."

Scrooge gruffly repeated the words, "Bah! Humbug."

"Don't be cross, Uncle," said the nephew.

"What else can I be," returned the uncle, "when I live in such a world of fools as this Merry Christmas! Out upon merry Christmas. What's Christmastime to you but a time for paying bills without money? What is it but a time for being a year older, but not an hour richer? If I had my way," said Scrooge indignantly, "every idiot who calls out "Merry Christmas" should be boiled and buried with a stake of holly through his heart. He should!"

"Uncle!" pleaded the nephew.

"Nephew!" returned the uncle, sternly, "keep Christmas in your own way, and let me keep it in mine."

"Keep it!" repeated Scrooge's nephew. "But you don't keep it."

"Let me leave it alone, then," said Scrooge. "Much good may it do you! Much good it has ever done you!"

"There are many things that make me glad but yield no profit," returned the nephew. "Christmas is one. I have always thought of Christmas as a kind, forgiving, charitable, pleasant time. It is the only time I know of when men and women open their shut-up hearts freely, and think of people less fortunate. And therefore, Uncle, though it has never put a scrap of gold or silver in my pocket, I believe that it *has* done me good, and *will* do me good. And I say, God bless it!"

The clerk applauded. Then, aware of displeasing Scrooge, he poked the fire and extinguished the last dim spark forever.

"Let me hear another sound from *you*," said Scrooge, "and you'll keep your Christmas by losing your job. You're quite a powerful speaker, sir," he added, turning to his nephew. "I wonder you don't go into Parliament."

"Don't be angry, Uncle. Come! Dine with us tomorrow."

Scrooge declined.

"But why?" cried Scrooge's nephew. "Why?"

"Why did you get married?" said Scrooge.

"Because I fell in love."

"Because you fell in love!" growled Scrooge, as if that were the only one thing in the world more ridiculous than a merry Christmas. "Good afternoon!"

"I want nothing from you. I ask nothing of you. Why cannot we be friends?"

"Good afternoon," said Scrooge.

"I am sorry, with all my heart, to find you so stubborn. We have never had any quarrel. But I'll keep my Christmas spirit to the last. So a merry Christmas, Uncle!"

"Good afternoon!" growled Scrooge.

"And a happy New Year!"

"Good afternoon!" Scrooge growled again.

His nephew left the room. He stopped at the outer door to wish a merry Christmas to the clerk, who, cold as he was, was warmer than Scrooge. The clerk returned the nephew's greetings cordially.

"Imagine," muttered Scrooge. "My clerk, who earns a meager fifteen shillings a week, and has a wife and family, talking about a merry Christmas. What insanity."

In letting Scrooge's nephew out, the clerk had let two other people in. These gentlemen, pleasant to behold, now stood, with their hats off, in Scrooge's office. They had books and papers in their hands, and they bowed to him.

"Scrooge and Marley's, I believe," said one of the gentlemen, referring to his list. "Have I the pleasure of addressing Mr. Scrooge, or Mr. Marley?"

"Mr. Marley has been dead these seven years," Scrooge replied. "He died seven years ago, this very night."

"We have no doubt his generosity is well represented by his surviving partner," said the gentleman, presenting his credentials.

At the ominous word "generosity," Scrooge frowned, and shook his head, and handed the credentials back.

"At this festive season of the year, Mr. Scrooge," said the gentleman, taking up a pen, "it is fitting that we should make some slight provision for the poor, who suffer greatly at the present time."

"Are there no prisons?" asked Scrooge.

"Plenty of prisons," said the gentleman, laying down the pen again.

"And the workhouses?" demanded Scrooge. "Are they still in operation?"

"They are. However, the prisons and the workhouses scarcely furnish Christian cheer of mind or body to the poverty-stricken," returned the gentleman. "A few of us are collecting money to buy the poor some meat and drink, and means of warmth. We choose this time, because it is a time, of all others, when Want is keenly felt, and Abundance rejoices. How much would you like to contribute?"

"Nothing!" Scrooge replied. "I don't make merry myself at Christmas, and I can't afford to make idle people merry. I help to support the establishments I have mentioned. They cost enough, and those who are badly off must go there."

"Many can't go there, and many would rather die."

"If they would rather die," said Scrooge, "they had better do it, and decrease the surplus population. Good afternoon, gentlemen!"

Seeing that it would be useless to argue further, the gentlemen withdrew. Scrooge resumed his labors, feeling more pleased with himself than usual.

Meanwhile the fog and darkness thickened. The ancient tower of a church became invisible. It struck the hours and quarters in the clouds, with vibrations afterward, as if its teeth were chattering in its frozen head. The cold became intense. In the street, some laborers had lighted a great fire in a large metal pan. A party of ragged men and boys were gathered round, warming their hands before the blaze.

Foggier yet, and colder! Piercing, searching, biting cold. One reveler, gnawed and numbed by the hungry cold as bones are gnawed by dogs, bent down at Scrooge's keyhole to entertain him with a Christmas carol. However, at the first sound of "God bless you, merry gentleman! May nothing you dismay!" Scrooge seized the ruler so energetically that the singer fled in terror, leaving the keyhole to the fog and frost.

At length the hour of shutting up the counting house arrived. With an ill will, Scrooge dismounted from his stool. Seeing this, the clerk instantly snuffed his candle out and put on his hat.

"You'll want tomorrow off, I suppose?" said Scrooge.

"If quite convenient, Sir."

"It's not convenient," said Scrooge, "and it's not fair. If I refused to pay you for it, you'd think yourself ill-used, I suppose?"

The clerk smiled faintly.

"And yet," said Scrooge, "you don't think *me* ill-used, when I pay a day's wages for no work."

The clerk observed that it was only once a year.

"A poor excuse for picking a man's pocket every twenty-fifth of December!" said Scrooge, buttoning his greatcoat to the chin. "But I suppose you must have the whole day. Be here all the earlier next morning!"

Scrooge took his melancholy dinner in his usual melancholy tavern and then went home to bed. He lived in an apartment that had once belonged to his deceased partner. It was a gloomy suite of rooms in a dark and dreary section of London.

There was nothing at all unusual about the knocker on the door, except that it was very large. Scrooge had seen it every night and morning. But tonight, Scrooge, as he put his key in the lock, saw in the knocker, not a knocker, but Marley's face.

Marley's face. It looked at Scrooge as Marley used to look, with ghostly spectacles turned up upon its ghostly forehead. The hair was curiously stirred, as if by breath or hot air. And, though the eyes were wide open, they were perfectly motionless. That, and its livid color, made it horribly frightening.

As Scrooge stared hard at this object, it became a knocker again.

He was startled. But he unlocked the door, walked in, and lighted his candle.

Up the gloomy staircase Scrooge went. Darkness is cheap, and Scrooge liked it. But before he shut his heavy door, he walked through his rooms to see that all was right.

Sitting room, bedroom, kitchen. All appeared as they should be. Nobody under the table, nobody under the sofa. A small fire in the grate. Nobody under the bed. Nobody in the closet. Nobody in his dressing gown, which was hanging up against the wall.

Quite satisfied, he closed the door and locked himself in. Indeed, he double-locked himself in, which was not his custom. Thus secured against surprise, he took off his necktie and put on his dressing gown and slippers and his nightcap. Thus attired, he sat down before the fire to eat some thin watery porridge.

There was a very low fire for such a bitter night. He had to sit close to it to feel the least sensation of warmth. As he sat down, a servant's bell—not used for many years—began to swing. It swung so softly at first that it scarcely made a sound, but soon it rang out loudly. So did every bell in the house.

This might have lasted half a minute, but it seemed an hour. The bells ceased as they had begun, together. They were succeeded by a clanking noise, deep down below, as if some person were dragging a heavy chain over the casks in the wine-merchant's shop on the first level.

The cellar door flew open with a booming sound, and then he heard the noise much louder, on the floors below; then coming up the stairs; then coming straight toward his door.

"It's humbug still!" said Scrooge. "I won't believe it."

His color changed though, when, without a pause, it came on through the heavy door, and passed into the room before his eyes. As it entered, the dying flame leaped up, as though it cried, "I know him! Marley's Ghost!" and fell again.

The same face, the very same. Marley in his pigtail, usual jacket, pants, and boots, with a folded kerchief around his head and chin. The chain he carried was clasped about his middle and wound about him like a tail. It was made (for Scrooge observed it closely) of cash-boxes, keys, padlocks, ledgers, deeds, and heavy purses wrought in steel. The Ghost's body was transparent, so that Scrooge, looking through his jacket, could see the two buttons on the back.

"How now!" said Scrooge, caustic and cold as ever. "What do you want with me?"

"Much!"—Marley's voice, no doubt about it.

"Who are you?"

"Ask me who I *was*."

"Who *were* you then?" said Scrooge, raising his voice. "You're particular, for a ghost."

"In life I was your partner, Jacob Marley."

"Can you—can you sit down?" asked Scrooge, looking doubtfully at him.

"I can."

"Do it, then."

The Ghost sat down on the opposite side of the fireplace.

"You don't believe in me," observed the Ghost.

"I don't," said Scrooge.

"What evidence would you have of my reality beyond that of your senses?"

"I don't know," said Scrooge.

"Why do you doubt your senses?"

"Because," said Scrooge, "a little thing affects them. A slight disorder of the stomach makes them fanciful. You may be an undigested bit of beef, a blot of mustard, a crumb of cheese, a fragment of an underdone potato. There's more of gravy than of grave about you, whatever you are!"

At this joke, the spirit raised a frightful cry, and shook its chain with a dreadful clanking noise. Scrooge, terrified, held tightly to his chair so that he would not faint. But how much greater was his horror, when the phantom removed its kerchief, and its lower jaw dropped upon its chest!

Scrooge fell upon his knees and clasped his hands before his face.

"Mercy!" he said. "Dreadful spirit, why do you trouble me?"

"Now tell me," replied the Ghost, "do you believe in me or not?"

"I do," said Scrooge. "I must. But why do spirits walk the earth, and why do they come to me?"

"It is required of every man," the Ghost returned, "that the spirit within him should walk abroad among his fellow men, and travel far and wide. And if that spirit goes not forth in life, it is condemned to do so after death. It is doomed to wander through the world—oh, woe is me!—and witness what it cannot share, but might have shared when alive, and turned to happiness!"

Again the specter raised a cry, and shook its chain, and wrung its shadowy hands.

"You are chained," said Scrooge, trembling. "Tell me why?"

"I wear the chain I forged in life," replied the Ghost. "I made it link by link, and yard by yard. I made it of my own free will, and of my own free will I wore it."

Scrooge trembled more and more.

"Do you know," pursued the Ghost, "the weight and length of the strong coil you bear yourself? It was as heavy and as long as this, seven Christmas Eves ago when my earthly form died. You have labored on your own chain, since. Now it is longer!"

Scrooge glanced about him on the floor, in the expectation of finding himself surrounded by a lengthy iron cable. But he could see nothing.

"Jacob," he said, imploringly, "tell me more. Speak comfort to me, Jacob."

"I have none to give," the Ghost replied. "Comfort goes to other kinds of men, not you. Nor can I tell you all I wish to say. A very little more is all that is permitted to me. I cannot linger anywhere. In life my spirit never roved beyond the narrow limits of our money-changing establishment. Weary journeys lie before me!

"At this time of the year," the specter went on, "I suffer most. When I was alive, why did I walk through crowds of fellow beings with my eyes turned down, never caring about the less fortunate?"

Scrooge was very much dismayed to hear the specter going on so. Thinking of his own life, he began to shiver.

"Hear me!" cried the Ghost. "My time is nearly gone."

"I will," said Scrooge. "But don't be hard upon me, Jacob! Pray!"

"How it is that I appear before you in a shape that you can see, I may not tell. I have sat invisible beside you many and many a day. I am here tonight to warn you that you can still escape my fate. That much I have arranged for you."

"You were always a good friend to me," said Scrooge. "Thank'ee!"

"You will be haunted," resumed the Ghost, "by three Spirits."

Scrooge's countenance fell almost as low as the Ghost's had done.

"Is that the chance and hope you mentioned, Jacob?" he demanded, in a faltering voice.

"It is."

"I—I think I'd rather not," said Scrooge.

"Without their visits," said the Ghost, "you cannot hope to avoid the path I tread. Expect the first tomorrow, when the bell tolls One."

"Couldn't I meet them all at once, and have it over with, Jacob?" hinted Scrooge.

"Expect the second on the next night at the same hour. The third upon the next night when the last stroke of Twelve has ceased to vibrate. Look to see me no more. And for your own sake, remember what has passed between us."

When it had said these words, the specter took its cloth wrapper from the table and bound it round its head, as before. When the jaws were brought together again, they made a sharp sound.

The Ghost walked backward from him. At every step it took, the window raised itself a little, so that when the specter reached it, it was wide open.

It beckoned Scrooge to approach, which he did. When they were within two paces of each other, Marley's Ghost held up its hand, warning him to come no nearer. Scrooge stopped. From outside the window, he heard wailings of lamentation and regret, all mixed together. The specter, after listening for a moment, joined in the mournful chorus. Then he floated out upon the bleak, dark night.

Scrooge followed to the window and looked out.

The air was filled with phantoms, wandering here and there in restless haste, and moaning as they went. Every one of them wore chains like Marley's Ghost. Scrooge recognized many of them. He had been quite familiar with one old ghost, with a monstrous iron safe attached to its ankle. This Spirit cried piteously at being unable to assist a wretched woman with an infant. All the ghosts wished to help people in need, but they had lost that power forever.

Whether these creatures faded into mist, or mist enshrouded them, he could not tell. But they and their spirit voices faded away, and the night became as it had been.

Scrooge closed the window and examined the door by which the Ghost had entered. He had locked it with his own hands, and the bolts were undisturbed. He tried to say "Humbug!" but stopped at the first syllable. He was exhausted from emotion, or work, or his glimpse of the Invisible World, or the conversation of the Ghost, or the lateness of the hour. So he went straight to bed, without undressing, and immediately fell asleep.

CHAPTER 2

The First of the Three Spirits

Ebenezer Scrooge was awakened by the chimes from a nearby church tower—a deep, dull, melancholy One. At that moment, light flashed in the room, and the curtains of his bed were drawn aside by an unearthly visitor.

It was a strange figure—like a child, but with the features of an old man. Its hair, which hung about its neck and down its back, was white. Yet its face was not wrinkled. Its arms were very long and muscular. Its legs and feet, most delicately formed, were bare. It wore a tunic of the purest white and held a branch of fresh green holly in its hand. But what made it stranger still was that a bright clear jet of light sprang from the crown of its head.

Even this, though, was not its strangest quality. The figure itself constantly changed its shape. First it was a thing with one arm, then with one leg, then with twenty legs, then a pair of legs without a head, then a head without a body. Then it would return to its original form. And then change again.

"Are you the Spirit, sir, whose coming was foretold to me?" asked Scrooge.

"I am!"

The voice was soft and gentle, as if it spoke from a distance.

"Who and what are you?" Scrooge demanded.

"I am the Ghost of Christmas Past."

"Long past?" inquired Scrooge.

"No. Your past."

Scrooge then inquired what business brought him there.

"Your welfare!" said the Ghost. The Spirit put out its strong hand and clasped Scrooge gently by the arm. "Rise, and walk with me!"

It would have been in vain for Scrooge to plead that the weather and the hour were not ideal for traveling; that his bed was warm, and the thermometer below freezing; that he was wearing only slippers, dressing gown, and nightcap; and that he had a cold. The grasp, though gentle as a woman's hand, was not to be resisted. As the Spirit moved toward the window, Scrooge cried out, "I am mortal and liable to fall."

"Bear but a touch of my hand *there*," said the Spirit, laying it upon his heart, "and you shall be supported in more than this!"

They passed through the wall and stood upon an open country road, with fields on either side. The city had entirely vanished. It was a clear, cold, winter day, with snow upon the ground.

"Good Heaven!" said Scrooge, clasping his hands together, as he looked about him. "I was born in this place. I was a boy here!"

The Spirit gazed upon him kindly. Scrooge

was conscious of a thousand odors floating in the air, each one connected with a thousand thoughts, and hopes, and joys, and cares long forgotten.

"Your lip is trembling," said the Ghost. "And what is that upon your cheek?"

Scrooge muttered, with an unusual catch in his voice, that it was a pimple, and begged the Ghost to lead him where he would.

"You recollect the way?" inquired the Spirit.

"Remember it?" cried Scrooge with fervor. "I could walk it blindfolded."

"Strange to have forgotten it for so many years!" observed the Ghost. "Let us go on."

They walked along the road. Scrooge recognized every gate, and post, and tree. A little market town appeared in the distance, with its bridge, its church, and its winding river. Some shaggy ponies were trotting toward them with boys upon their backs, who called to other boys in country wagons and carts. All these boys were in great spirits, and shouted to each other, until the broad fields were so full of merry music, that the crisp air laughed to hear it.

"These are but shadows of the things that have been," said the Ghost. "They have no awareness of us."

The joyful travelers approached. Scrooge knew and named every one of them. Why did his cold eye glisten, and his heart leap up as they went past? Why was he filled with gladness when he heard them wish each other Merry Christmas? What was Merry Christmas to Scrooge? What good had it ever done to him?

"The school is not quite deserted," said the Ghost. "A solitary child, neglected by his friends, is left there still."

Scrooge said he knew it. And he sobbed.

They left the road, by a well-remembered lane, and soon approached a structure of dull red brick. The rooms were poorly furnished. A chilly bareness seemed to define the place. All about it was the suggestion of too much getting up by candlelight, and not too much to eat.

The Ghost and Scrooge went to a door at the back of the building. It opened before them, and disclosed a long, bare, melancholy room. At a desk sat a lonely boy, reading, near a feeble fire. Scrooge wept to see his poor forgotten self as he used to be.

"I wish," Scrooge muttered, putting his hand in his pocket, and looking about him, after drying his eyes with his cuff. "But it's too late now."

"What is the matter?" asked the Spirit.

"Nothing," said Scrooge. "Nothing. There was a boy singing a Christmas carol at my door last night. I wish I had given him something. That's all."

The Ghost smiled thoughtfully, and waved

its hand, saying as it did so, "Let us see another Christmas!"

Scrooge's former self grew larger at the words, and the room became a little darker and dirtier. The panels shrank; the windows cracked. Fragments of plaster fell from the ceiling. How all this was brought about, Scrooge did not know. He only knew that there he was, alone again, when all the other boys had gone home for the jolly holidays.

He was not reading now, but walking up and down despairingly. Scrooge looked at the Ghost, and with a mournful shaking of his head, glanced anxiously toward the door.

It opened, and a little girl, much younger than the boy, came darting in. She put her arms about his neck and kissed him on the cheek.

"I have come to bring you home, dear brother!" said the child, clapping her tiny hands, and bending down to laugh. "To bring you home, home, home!"

"Home, little Fan?" returned the boy.

"Yes!" said the child, happily. "Home, forever and ever. Father is so much kinder than he used to be that home's like Heaven! He spoke so gently to me one night when I was going to bed, that I was not afraid to ask him once more if you might come home. And he said Yes, you should. So he sent me in a coach to bring you," said the child. "And you are never to come back here. But first, we're to be together for all of Christmas and have the merriest time in all the world."

"You are quite a girl, little Fan!" exclaimed the boy.

She clapped her hands and laughed, and stood on tiptoe to embrace him. Then she began to drag him, in her childish eagerness, toward the door. They soon climbed into the coach and sped away from the school.

"She was a delicate creature," said the Ghost. "But she had a large heart!"

"So she had," cried Scrooge.

"She died a young woman," said the Ghost, "and had, I think, children."

"One child," Scrooge responded.

"True," said the Ghost. "Your nephew!"

Scrooge seemed troubled, and answered briefly, "Yes."

They had left the school behind them. Now they were in the busy streets of a city. People passed to and fro, while carts and coaches did battle in the streets. The windows of the shops made clear that here, too, it was Christmastime again.

The Ghost stopped at a warehouse door and asked Scrooge if he knew it.

"Know it!" said Scrooge. "I was apprenticed here!"

They went in and beheld an old gentleman

in a wig, sitting behind a high desk. Scrooge cried in great excitement, "Why, it's old Fezziwig! Bless his heart. It's Fezziwig alive again!"

Old Fezziwig laid down his pen and looked up at the clock, whose hands pointed to seven in the evening. He rubbed his hands, adjusted his jacket, and called out, "Yo ho, there! Ebenezer! Dick!"

Scrooge's former self, now a young man, came briskly in, accompanied by his fellow apprentice.

"Dick Wilkins, to be sure!" said Scrooge to the Ghost. "Bless me, yes. He was very much attached to me, was Dick. Poor Dick! Dear, dear!"

"Yo ho, my boys!" said Fezziwig. "No more work tonight. Christmas Eve, Dick. Christmas, Ebenezer! Let's have the shutters up," cried old Fezziwig, with a sharp clap of his hands.

They charged into the street with the shutters, placed and barred and pinned them, and came back, panting like racehorses.

"Hi-ho!" cried old Fezziwig, skipping down from the high desk, with wonderful agility. "Clear away, my lads, and let's have lots of room here! We're going to celebrate!"

Clear away! In a minute, all articles of business were put away. Fuel was heaped upon the fire. The warehouse was as snug, and warm, and dry, and bright as a ballroom.

In came a fiddler with a music book. In came Mrs. Fezziwig, one vast substantial smile. In came the three Miss Fezziwigs, beaming and lovable. In came the six young suitors whose hearts they broke. In came all the young men and women employed in the business. In came the housemaid, with her cousin, the baker. In came the cook, with her brother's particular friend, the milkman. The fiddler fiddled, and all the guests danced 'round. Cold meats were set out, with mince pies, cakes, and plenty of beer.

When the clock struck eleven, this domestic ball broke up. Mr. and Mrs. Fezziwig shook hands with every person individually as he or she went out and wished him or her a Merry Christmas. The apprentices were the last to leave.

During all this time, Scrooge had acted like a man out of his wits. He remembered everything, enjoyed everything, and felt a great excitement. It was not until now, when the bright faces of his former self and Dick were turned from them, that he remembered the Ghost. Scrooge became conscious that it was looking directly at him, while the light upon its head burned very clearly.

"A small expense," said the Ghost, "to make these silly folks so full of joy and gratitude."

"Small!" echoed Scrooge.

The Spirit motioned to him to listen to the two apprentices, who were repeatedly praising Fezziwig. When they became silent, the Ghost exclaimed, "Fezziwig has spent but a few pounds, three or four perhaps. Is that so much that he deserves this praise?"

"It isn't that," said Scrooge, angered by the remark. "He has the power to make our work a pleasure or a toil. The happiness he gives is as great as if it cost a fortune."

He felt the Spirit's glance, and stopped.

"What is the matter?" asked the Ghost.

"Nothing," said Scrooge.

"Something, I think?" the Ghost insisted.

"No," said Scrooge, "No. I should like to be able to say a word or two to my clerk just now! That's all."

His former self turned down the lamps, and Scrooge and the Ghost again stood side by side in the open air.

"My time grows short," observed the Spirit. "Quick!"

Now Scrooge saw himself after several years. He was in the prime of life. His face did not have the harsh and rigid lines of later years, but it had begun to show the signs of care and greed.

He sat by the side of a fair young girl in a mourning dress. Tears were in her eyes.

"It matters little," she said, softly. "To you, very little. Another idol has taken my place."

"What idol?" he inquired.

"A golden one. I have seen your nobler aspirations fall off one by one, until the master-passion, Gain, absorbs you. Have I not?"

"Even if I have grown so much wiser, what then?" Scrooge replied. "I am not changed toward you."

She shook her head.

"Am I?"

"Our promise to love each other is an old one. It was made when we were both poor and content to be so. You *are* changed. When it was made, you were another man."

"I was a boy," he said impatiently.

"If we had never promised to be true to each other, when young," said the girl, "tell me, would you seek me out and try to win me now, when I am still penniless? Ah, no! I release you, for the love of him you once were. May you be happy in the life you have chosen!"

She left him, and they parted.

"Spirit!" said Scrooge, "show me no more! Why do you delight in torturing me?"

"One shadow more!" exclaimed the Ghost.

"No more!" cried Scrooge. "I don't wish to see it. Show me no more!"

But the relentless Ghost grasped him firmly and forced him to observe.

They were in another room, not large or handsome, but full of comfort. Near the winter fire sat a beautiful young girl, so like the last one that Scrooge believed it was the same. Then he saw *her*, now a mother, sitting opposite her daughter. There were more children there than Scrooge, in his agitated state of mind, could count. The noise in this room was tumultuous, but no one seemed to care. On the contrary, the mother and daughter laughed heartily and enjoyed it very much.

But now there was a knocking at the door. The father entered, laden with Christmas toys and presents. The children rushed at him. They dove into his pockets, relieved him of brown-paper parcels, hugged him round the neck, pounded his back, and kicked his legs in over-flowing affection! The shouts of wonder and delight with which the giving-out of every package was received! The joy, and gratitude, and ecstasy! At length the excitement subsided. One step at a time, the younger children trooped upstairs and went to bed.

And now Scrooge looked on more attentively than ever. There was the master of the house, his daughter leaning fondly on him, the mother close by. Scrooge realized that he might have been the father in that precious scene. A tear dimmed his eyesight.

"Belle," said the husband, turning to his wife with a smile, "I saw an old friend of yours this afternoon."

"Who was it?"

"Guess!"

"How can I? . . . I know," she added in the same breath, laughing as he laughed. "Mr. Scrooge."

"Mr. Scrooge it was. I passed his office window and saw him inside. His partner lies upon the point of death, I hear. Scrooge sat alone. Quite alone in the world, I do believe."

"Spirit!" said Scrooge in a broken voice, "remove me from this place."

"I told you these were shadows of the things that have been," said the Ghost. "They are what they are. Do not blame me!"

"Remove me!" Scrooge exclaimed, "I cannot bear it!"

He turned upon the Ghost and exclaimed, "Leave me! Take me back. Haunt me no longer!"

The Ghost's time was up. Scrooge was exhausted. An irresistible drowsiness overcame him. He was again in his own bedroom, where he sank into a heavy sleep.

CHAPTER 3
The Second of the Three Spirits

Awakened by his own thunderous snore, Scrooge sat up in bed to collect his thoughts. He was determined to challenge the second Spirit as soon as it appeared.

Being well prepared, he trembled violently when the church bell struck One, but no shape appeared. Five minutes, ten minutes, a quarter of an hour went by, yet nothing came. But there was a blaze of light—more alarming than a dozen ghosts. This ghostly light seemed to come from the adjoining room. Scrooge got up softly and shuffled in his slippers to the door.

The moment Scrooge's hand was on the lock, a strange voice called him by his name, and told him to enter. He obeyed.

It was his own room. There was no doubt about that. But it had undergone a surprising transformation. The walls and ceiling were so hung with living green that the room resembled a grove of trees. Bright gleaming berries glistened from every limb. Crisp leaves of holly, mistletoe, and ivy reflected the light, as if little mirrors had been scattered there. A mighty blaze was roaring in the fireplace. Heaped up on the floor, to form a kind of throne, were cooked turkeys, geese, game, poultry, great joints of meat, suckling pigs, long wreaths of sausages, mince pies, plum puddings, barrels of oysters, red-hot chestnuts, cherry-cheeked apples, juicy oranges, luscious pears, immense cakes, and bubbling bowls of punch. Upon this couch there sat a jolly Giant. He bore a glowing torch shaped like a horn of plenty. The Ghost held it up to shed its light on Scrooge.

"Come in!" exclaimed the Ghost. "Come in and know me better, man!"

Scrooge entered timidly and bowed his head before this Spirit. Though the Spirit's eyes were clear and kind, he did not like to meet them.

"I am the Ghost of Christmas Present," said the Spirit. "Look upon me!"

Scrooge obediently did so. It was clothed in a simple green robe, bordered with white fur. This garment hung so loosely on the figure that its broad chest was mostly bare. Its feet were also bare. On its head it wore a holly wreath, set here and there with shining icicles. Its dark brown curls were long and free—free as its friendly face, its sparkling eye, its open hand, its cheery voice, and its joyful air. Tied round its middle was an antique scabbard. However, no sword was in it, and the ancient sheath was eaten up with rust.

"You have never seen the like of me before!" exclaimed the Spirit.

"Never," Scrooge replied.

The Ghost stood. "Spirit," said Scrooge submissively, "conduct me where you will. I went forth last night against my will, and I learned a lesson that is working now. Tonight, if you have anything to teach me, let me profit by it."

"Touch my robe!"

Scrooge did as he was told.

Holly, mistletoe, red berries, ivy, turkeys, geese, game, poultry, meat, pigs, sausages, oysters, pies, puddings, fruit, and punch, all vanished instantly. So did the room, the fire, the ruddy glow, the hour of night. Instead, they stood in the city streets on a cold Christmas morning. People were scraping the snow from the pavement in front of their dwellings.

The house fronts looked black enough, and the windows blacker, contrasting with the smooth white sheet of snow upon the roofs, and with the dirtier snow upon the ground. The sky was gloomy, and the shortest streets were choked with a dingy mist, half thawed, half frozen. Soot from countless chimneys darkened the ground. Indeed, there was nothing very cheerful in the weather or the town. Yet there was an air of cheerfulness that the clearest summer air and brightest summer sun could not have fashioned.

For the people who were shoveling were happy. They called to one another and occasionally threw snowballs with every intention of missing. The poultry and grocery shops were still open. Eager customers were tumbling up against each other at the doors, some rushing in, others scrambling out.

But soon the church bells called the people. Off they went, flocking through the streets in their best clothes and happiest faces. At the same time, other people were carrying their uncooked dinners to the bakers' shops, where the food would be cooked for them. The sight of these impoverished citizens appeared to interest the Spirit very much. He stood, with Scrooge beside him, in a baker's doorway and sprinkled incense on their dinners from his torch. And it was a very unusual torch. Once or twice, when there were angry words between some dinner carriers who had pushed each other, he shed a few drops of water on them from it. Immediately, their good humor was restored. For, they said, it was a shame to quarrel on Christmas Day. And so it was!

"Is there a peculiar flavor in what you sprinkle from your torch?" asked Scrooge.

"There is. My own."

"Would it apply to any kind of dinner on this day?" asked Scrooge.

"To any kindly given. To a poor one most."

"Why to a poor one most?" asked Scrooge.

"Because it needs it most."

Perhaps it was the Spirit's kind, generous, hearty nature, and his sympathy with all poor men, that led him to Scrooge's clerk's dwelling. On the threshold, the Spirit smiled and stopped to bless Bob Cratchit's home—only four rooms—with the sprinkling of his torch.

There was Mrs. Cratchit, clothed but poorly in a twice-mended gown. But she had fastened ribbons to it. Ribbons cost little, but they make a pretty show. The good woman spread out the tablecloth, assisted by Belinda Cratchit, second of her daughters, also bedecked in ribbons. Son Peter Cratchit plunged a fork into the saucepan of potatoes. And now two smaller Cratchits, boy and girl, came tearing in, screaming that outside the baker's they had smelled the goose, and known it for their own. Anticipating the delights of Christmas dinner, these young Cratchits danced about the table.

"What's keeping your precious father?" said Mrs. Cratchit. "And where is your brother, Tiny Tim? And Martha wasn't as late last Christmas Day by half an hour!"

"Here's Martha, Mother!" cried the two young Cratchits. "Hurrah! Martha!"

"Why, bless your heart alive, my dear, how late you are!" said Mrs. Cratchit, kissing Martha a dozen times, and taking off her shawl and bonnet for her with a great fuss.

"We'd a deal of work to finish up last

night," replied the girl, "and had to clear away this morning, Mother!"

"Well! Never mind, so long as you are here," said Mrs. Cratchit. "Sit down before the fire, my dear, and get yourself warm, Lord bless you!"

"No, no! There's Father coming," cried the two young Cratchits, who were everywhere at once. "Hide, Martha, hide!"

So Martha hid herself, and in came little Bob and his father. The latter's threadbare clothes were mended and brushed. Tiny Tim sat upon his shoulder. Alas for Tiny Tim, he carried a little crutch, and his limbs were supported by an iron frame!

"Why, where's our Martha?" cried Bob Cratchit, looking around.

"Not coming," said Mrs. Cratchit.

"Not coming?" said Bob, with a sudden decline in his high spirits. "Not coming upon Christmas Day?"

Martha didn't like to see him disappointed. She rushed out from behind the closet door and ran into his arms. Meanwhile, the two young Cratchits carried Tiny Tim to the kitchen, so that he might hear the pudding bubbling in the pot.

"And how did little Tim behave?" asked Mrs. Cratchit, when Bob had hugged his daughter to his heart's content.

"As good as gold," said Bob, "and better. Somehow he gets thoughtful, sitting by himself so much, and thinks the strangest things you ever heard. He told me, coming home, that he hoped the people saw him in the church, because he was a cripple. The sight of him might remind them, upon Christmas Day, who it was that made lame beggars walk, and blind men see."

Bob's voice trembled when he told them this, and trembled more when he said that Tiny Tim was growing strong and hearty.

His active little crutch was heard upon the floor, and back came Tiny Tim, escorted by his brother and sister. Bob, meanwhile, prepared a hot mixture in a jug with gin and lemons, and put it by the fire to simmer. Peter and the two young Cratchits went to fetch the goose, with which they soon returned in high spirits.

Such a commotion followed that you might have thought a goose the rarest of all birds, compared to which a swan was quite ordinary. And in truth, a goose was rarely found in that poor house. Mrs. Cratchit made the gravy (in a little saucepan) hissing hot. Master Peter mashed the potatoes with incredible vigor. Miss Belinda sweetened up the applesauce. Martha dusted the hot plates. The two young Cratchits set chairs for everybody. At last the dishes were brought out, and grace was said. It was followed by a breathless pause, as Mrs. Cratchit, prepared to plunge the carving knife into the goose. When she did, and when the long-expected gush of stuffing issued forth, a murmur of delight arose all around the table. Even Tiny Tim beat on the table with the handle of his knife, and feebly cried "Hurrah!"

There never was such a goose! Its tenderness and flavor, size and cheapness, were universally admired. Accompanied by applesauce and mashed potatoes, it was a sufficient dinner for the whole family.

But there was more to come. Mrs. Cratchit left the room and then returned, flushed, but smiling proudly. To the table she carried the dessert pudding, looking like a speckled cannonball, so hard and firm, blazing in flaming brandy, and decorated with Christmas holly stuck into the top.

Oh, what a wonderful pudding! Bob Cratchit said that it was the greatest success achieved by Mrs. Cratchit since their marriage.

At last the dinner was done, the cloth was cleared, the hearth swept, and the fire tended to. The mixture in the jug was tasted, and considered perfect. Apples and oranges were put upon the table, and a shovelful of chestnuts on the fire. Then all the Cratchit family drew round the hearth. At Bob Cratchit's elbow stood the family store of glassware—two tumblers and a custard cup without a handle.

Bob filled these with the hot liquid from the jug, while the chestnuts on the fire sputtered and cracked noisily. Then Bob proposed: "A Merry Christmas to us all, my dears. God bless us!" Which all the family re-echoed.

"God bless us every one!" said Tiny Tim, the last of all.

He sat very close to his father's side upon his little stool. Bob held his withered little hand in his, as if he feared Tiny Tim might be taken from him.

"Spirit," said Scrooge, with an interest he had never felt before, "tell me if Tiny Tim will live."

"I see a vacant seat," replied the Ghost, "in the poor chimney corner, and a crutch without an owner, carefully preserved. If these shadows remain unaltered by the Future, the child will die."

"No, no," said Scrooge. "Oh, no, kind Spirit! Say he will be spared."

"If these shadows remain unaltered by the Future, none other of my race," returned the Ghost, "will find him here. What then? If he is likely to die, he had better do it, and decrease the surplus population."

Scrooge hung his head to hear his own words quoted by the Spirit, and was overcome with shame and grief. But then he raised his head abruptly on hearing his own name.

"Mr. Scrooge!" said Bob. "A toast to Mr. Scrooge, the Founder of the Feast!"

"The Founder of the Feast indeed!" cried Mrs. Cratchit. "I wish I had him here. I'd give him a piece of my mind to feast upon."

"My dear," said Bob, "the children. It's Christmas Day."

"It should be Christmas Day, I am sure," said she, "on which one drinks the health of such a hateful, stingy, hard, unfeeling man as Mr. Scrooge. You know he is, Robert! Nobody knows it better than you do, poor fellow!"

"My dear," was Bob's mild answer, "Christmas Day."

"I'll drink his health for your sake and the Day's," said Mrs. Cratchit, "not for his. Long life to him. A merry Christmas and a happy New Year! He'll be very merry and very happy, I have no doubt!"

The children drank the toast after her. It was the first of their proceedings that had no heartiness. Scrooge was an evil monster to the family. The mention of his name cast a dark shadow on the party, which did not disappear for a full five minutes.

After it had passed away, they were ten times merrier than before, relieved that any mention of Scrooge was finished. Bob Cratchit told them how he had a job prospect for Master Peter, who would earn, if he was hired, five shillings and sixpence weekly. The two young Cratchits laughed tremendously at the idea of Peter's being a man of business. Martha, who was a poor apprentice at a milliner's, then told everyone about her work and its long hours. All this time the chestnuts and the jug went round and round.

There was nothing remarkable in this. They were not a handsome family. Their clothes were shabby; their shoes were no longer waterproof. But they were happy, grateful, and pleased with one another. Scrooge gazed at them, and especially at Tiny Tim, until the last.

By this time it was getting dark and snowing heavily. And as Scrooge and the Spirit went along the streets, the brightness of the roaring fires in kitchens, parlors, and all sorts of rooms, was wonderful. Here, the flickering of the blaze showed preparations for a cozy dinner, with hot plates baking before the fire, and red curtains, ready to be drawn to shut out cold and darkness. There, all the children of the house were running out into the snow to be the first to greet their married sisters, brothers, cousins, uncles, aunts. Over there a group of handsome girls, all hooded and fur-booted, tripped lightly off to some near neighbor's house.

If you had judged from the numbers of people on their way to friendly gatherings, you might have thought that no one was at home to give them welcome when they got there. But instead, every house expected company, and piled up its fires half-chimney high. Blessings on it, how the Ghost exulted! How it sprinkled its mirth on everything within its reach!

Suddenly, they stood on a bleak and deserted plain. Even here, Christmas was being celebrated. In a poor miner's cottage, a merry family was gathered, singing a Christmas song. Then the Spirit told Scrooge to hold his robe, and they sped to the sea. In a solitary lighthouse, two men who guarded the light had made a fire and wished each other Merry Christmas. Upon a ship far out at sea, the crew shared tales of past Christmas celebrations with family and friends.

It was a great surprise to Scrooge, listening to the moaning of the wind and sea, to hear a hearty laugh. It was a much greater surprise to Scrooge to recognize it as his own nephew's. He was in a bright, dry, gleaming room, with the Spirit standing smiling by his side.

There is nothing in the world so irresistibly contagious as laughter. When Scrooge's nephew laughed, holding his sides, rolling his head, and twisting his face into the most extravagant contortions, Scrooge's niece, by marriage, laughed as heartily as he. And their assembled friends roared out lustily, "Ha, ha! Ha, ha, ha, ha!"

"He said that Christmas was a humbug, as I live!" cried Scrooge's nephew.

"More shame for him, Fred!" said Scrooge's niece, indignantly.

"He's a comical old fellow," said Scrooge's nephew, "that's the truth. And he's not so terribly pleasant, either. However, his offenses carry their own punishment. I have nothing to say against him."

"I'm sure he is very rich, Fred," hinted Scrooge's niece.

"What of that, my dear!" said Scrooge's nephew. "His wealth is of no use to him. He doesn't do any good with it. He doesn't make himself comfortable with it. He hasn't the satisfaction of thinking—ha, ha, ha!—that he is ever going to benefit *us* with it."

"I have no patience with him," observed Scrooge's niece. Scrooge's niece's sisters, and all the other ladies, expressed the same opinion.

"Oh, I have!" said Scrooge's nephew. "I am sorry for him. I couldn't be angry with him if I tried. Who suffers by his ill whims? Himself, always. He has decided to dislike us, and he won't come and dine with us. What's the consequence? He doesn't lose much of a dinner."

"Indeed, I think he loses a very good dinner," interrupted Scrooge's niece.

"I was only going to say," said Scrooge's nephew, "that he loses some pleasant moments, which could do him no harm. I mean to give him the same chance every year, whether he likes it or not, for I pity him. He may laugh at Christmas till he dies. But he can't help thinking better of it—I defy him—if he finds me going there, in good temper, year after year, and saying 'Uncle Scrooge, how are you?'"

After tea, they sang songs, and Scrooge's niece played the harp. Then they played games, posing riddles for each other. There might have been twenty people there, young and old, but they all played, and so did Scrooge. Forgetting that his voice made no sound in their ears, he sometimes made his guess quite loud, and very often guessed quite right, too.

The Ghost was greatly pleased to find him in this mood, and looked upon him with such favor, that Scrooge begged to be allowed to stay until the guests departed. But the Spirit said this could not be done.

"Here is a new game," said Scrooge. "One half hour, Spirit, only one!"

It was a game called "Yes and No." Scrooge's nephew thought of something, and the rest had to find out what it was. He could answer their questions only by saying yes or no. Soon they learned that he was thinking of an animal, a live animal, a rather disagreeable animal, a savage animal, an animal that growled and grunted sometimes, and talked sometimes, and lived in London, and walked about the streets, and wasn't led by anybody on a leash, and didn't live in a zoo, and was never killed in a market, and was not a horse, or a donkey, or a cow, or a bull, or a tiger, or a dog, or a pig, or a cat, or a bear. At every fresh question that was put to him, the nephew burst into a fresh roar of laughter.

At last one sister cried out, "I have found it out! I know what it is, Fred!"

"What is it?" cried Fred.

"It's your Uncle Scro-o-o-o-oge!"

Which it certainly was. Everyone applauded, though some objected that the reply to "Is it a bear?" ought to have been "Yes."

"He has given us plenty of merriment, I am sure," said Fred, "and it would be ungrateful not to drink his health. Here is a glass of mulled wine, and I say, 'Uncle Scrooge!'"

"Well! Uncle Scrooge," they cried.

"A merry Christmas and a happy New Year to the old man, whatever he is!" said Scrooge's nephew.

Uncle Scrooge had become so light of heart that he would have toasted the company in return if the Ghost had given him time. But he and the Spirit were again upon their travels.

Much they saw, and far they went, and many homes they visited, but always with a happy end. The Spirit stood beside sick beds, and the sick became cheerful. In poorhouse, hospital, and jail, in misery's every refuge, he left his blessing and taught Scrooge his beliefs.

It was a long night. The Christmas holiday season appeared to be condensed into the time they spent together. It was strange, too, that while Scrooge's appearance did not change, the Ghost grew older. Scrooge had observed this change, but never spoke of it, until they left a children's Twelfth Night party. Looking at the Spirit as they stood together in an open place, he noticed that its hair was gray.

"Are spirits' lives so short?" asked Scrooge.

"My life upon this globe is very brief," replied the Ghost. "It ends tonight."

"Tonight!" cried Scrooge.

"Tonight at midnight. Hark! The time is drawing near." The chimes were ringing three quarters past eleven at that moment.

"Forgive me if I am not justified in what I ask," said Scrooge, looking intently at the Spirit's robe, "but I see something strange beneath your skirts."

From the folds of its robe, the Spirit brought out two children. They were wretched, sad, hideous, miserable. They knelt down at its feet and clung to the outside of its garment.

They were a boy and girl. Yellow, sickly, ragged, scowling, wolfish, but respectful of the Spirit. The grace of youth should have filled out their faces and tinted them with a rosy glow. But a stale and shriveled hand had pinched and twisted them, and pulled them into shreds.

Scrooge started back, appalled. He tried to say they were fine children, but the words died in his throat.

"Spirit! Are they yours?" Scrooge could say no more.

"They are Man's," said the Spirit, looking down upon them. "This boy is Ignorance. This girl is Want. Beware them both, but most of all beware the boy. On his brow I see written the word Doom, unless the writing be erased. Deny it, and make it worse!" cried the Spirit, stretching out its hand toward the city. "If you ignore those who warn you, beware the consequences!"

"Have they no refuge or resource?" cried Scrooge.

"Are there no prisons?" said the Spirit, turning on him for the last time with his own words. "Are there no workhouses?"

The bell struck twelve.

Scrooge looked around for the Ghost. It was gone. As the last stroke ceased to vibrate, he beheld a solemn Phantom, draped and hooded, coming, like a mist along the ground, toward him.

CHAPTER 4
The Last of the Spirits

The Phantom slowly, gravely, silently approached. When it came, Scrooge kneeled. The very air through which this Spirit moved seemed marked by gloom and mystery.

It was shrouded in a deep black garment, which concealed its form. Nothing of it was visible except for one outstretched hand. Except for this, it would have been difficult to separate it from the darkness surrounding it. The Spirit's mysterious presence filled Scrooge with a solemn dread.

"I am in the presence of the Ghost of Christmas Yet To Come?" asked Scrooge.

The Spirit did not answer, but pointed onward.

"You are about to show me what will happen in the time before us," Scrooge pursued. "Is that so, Spirit?"

The upper portion of the garment rustled, as if the Spirit had inclined its head.

Although well used to ghostly company by this time, Scrooge feared the silent shape so much that his legs trembled. When he prepared to follow it, he could hardly stand. The Spirit paused a moment, giving him time to recover.

But Scrooge was all the worse for this. It

horrified him to know that behind the dusky shroud, there were ghostly eyes fixed upon him. Scrooge, for his part, could see nothing but a ghostly hand and one great heap of black.

"Ghost of the Future!" he exclaimed. "I fear you more than any specter I have seen. But I know your purpose is to do me good. And I hope to live to be a different man than what I was. Therefore, I am prepared to go with you, and do it with a thankful heart. Will you not speak to me?"

It did not reply. Its hand pointed straight ahead.

"Lead on!" said Scrooge. "The night is fading fast, and it is precious time to me, I know. Lead on, Spirit!"

The Phantom moved away. Scrooge followed in the shadow of its robe, which bore him up and carried him along.

They scarcely seemed to enter the city. Rather, the city seemed to spring up about them. They found themselves in the middle of the business district.

The Spirit stopped beside one little knot of businessmen. Scrooge saw that its hand was pointed at them, so he advanced to listen to their talk.

"No," said a fat man with a monstrous chin, "I don't know much about it. I only know he's dead."

"When did he die?" inquired another.

"Last night, I believe."

"Why, what was the matter with him?" asked a third. "I thought he'd never die."

"God knows," said the first, with a yawn.

"What has he done with his money?" asked a red-faced gentleman with an enormous nose.

"I haven't heard," said the man with the large chin, yawning again. "Left it to his company, perhaps. He hasn't left it to *me*. That's all I know."

This pleasantry was received with a general laugh.

"It's likely to be a very cheap funeral," said the same speaker. "I don't know of anybody who would go to it. Shall we volunteer?"

"I don't mind going if a lunch is provided," observed the gentleman with the large nose. "But I must be fed, if I am to attend."

Another laugh.

The three men strolled away. Scrooge knew the men and looked toward the Spirit for an explanation.

The Phantom glided on into a street. Its finger pointed to two persons. Scrooge listened again, thinking that the explanation might lie here.

He knew these men, also. They were men of business, very wealthy, and of great importance. He had been nice to them, for business purposes.

"Well!" said the first. "Old Scratch has got his own at last, hey?"

"So I am told," returned the second. "Cold, isn't it?"

"Seasonable for Christmastime."

Not another word. That was their meeting, their conversation, and their parting.

Scrooge was surprised that the Spirit should attach importance to such trivial conversations. He wondered what they might mean. They could not concern the death of Jacob, his old partner, for that was Past, and this Ghost's realm was the Future. He looked for his own image, but another man stood in his usual place.

The Phantom beckoned to him. They went into a part of the town where Scrooge had never been before. The streets were foul and narrow. The shops and houses were wretched. The people wore rags and were drunken, diseased and ugly. The whole quarter reeked with crime and filth and misery.

In the midst of this foul-smelling squalor, there was a little shop. Upon its floor were piled up heaps of rusty keys, nails, chains, hinges, files, scales, weights, and other odds and ends. Sitting among these products, by a charcoal stove, was a gray-haired merchant of some seventy years. Three customers, each with a heavy bundle, were in the shop: a housekeeper, a laundress, and an undertaker's assistant.

"What a coincidence, old Joe, for us three to meet here!" said one of the customers.

"You couldn't have met in a better place," said old Joe, the proprietor, removing his pipe from his mouth. "Come into the parlor."

The parlor was the space behind a screen of hanging rags. The old man raked the fire, while one of the women exclaimed, "Every person has a right to take care of themselves. *He* always did!"

The other woman spoke. "Who's the worse for the loss of a few things like these? Not a dead man, I suppose. Open that bundle, old Joe, and let me know its value."

Before Old Joe took another draw on his pipe, the other customers revealed their treasures. The undertaker's assistant, appropriately dressed in faded black, produced a pencil case, a pair of sleeve-buttons, and a brooch of no great value. They were carefully examined and appraised by old Joe, who chalked the sums he would pay for each item upon the wall.

"That's your account," said Joe, "and I wouldn't give another sixpence. Who's next?"

The laundress revealed some sheets and towels, a little wearing apparel, two old-fashioned silver teaspoons, a pair of sugar tongs, and a few boots. Her account was placed on the wall in the same manner.

"I always give too much to ladies. It's a

weakness of mine, and that's the way I ruin myself," said old Joe.

"And now undo *my* bundle, Joe," said the housekeeper.

Joe went down on his knees to open it, and having unfastened a great many knots, dragged out a large and heavy roll of dark fabric.

"What do you call this?" said Joe. "Bed curtains?"

The woman nodded.

"You don't mean to say you took them down, rings and all, with him lying there?" said Joe.

"Yes, I do," replied the woman. "Why not?"

"You were born to make your fortune," said Joe, "and you'll certainly do it."

"I certainly shan't restrain myself for the sake of such a man as He was, I promise you, Joe," returned the woman coolly. "Don't drop that oil upon the blankets, now."

"His blankets?" asked Joe.

"Whose else's do you think?" replied the woman. "He isn't likely to catch cold without 'em, I dare say."

"I hope he didn't die of anything contagious?" said old Joe, stopping in his work, and looking up.

"Don't you be afraid of that," returned the woman. "I wouldn't linger near him for such things, if he did. Ah! you may look through that shirt till your eyes ache. But you won't find a hole in it, nor a threadbare place. It's the best he had, and a fine one too. They'd have wasted it, if it hadn't been for me."

"What do you call wasting it?" asked old Joe.

"Putting it on him to be buried in, to be sure," replied the woman with a laugh. "Somebody was fool enough to do it, but I took it off again. He can't look uglier in a cheap shirt than he did in the good one."

Scrooge listened to this dialogue in horror. As they sat in the dim light of the old man's lamp, Scrooge viewed them with hatred and disgust.

"Spirit!" said Scrooge, shuddering from head to foot. "I see, I see. The case of this unhappy man might be my own. Merciful Heaven, what is this!"

He recoiled in terror, for the scene had changed. He was standing in a dark room. A pale light fell straight upon a bare bed. On it, covered with a ragged sheet, was the body of a man.

Scrooge glanced toward the Phantom. Its steady hand pointed to the head. The cover was so carelessly adjusted that the slightest motion of a finger would have revealed the face. He longed to do it, but found himself unable.

The lifeless body lay alone in the dark empty house. Not a man, a woman, or a child, was there to say that he was good or kind. A cat was tearing at the door, and there was a sound of gnawing rats beneath the hearthstone. What *they* wanted in the room of death, and why they were so restless and disturbed, Scrooge did not dare to think.

"Spirit!" he said, "this is a fearful place. In leaving it, I shall not leave its lesson. Let us go!"

Still the Ghost pointed to the head.

"I understand you," Scrooge returned, "and I would do it, if I could. But I have not the power, Spirit."

Again it seemed to look upon him.

"If there is any person in the town, who feels emotion caused by this man's death," said Scrooge, quite agonized, "show that person to me, Spirit, I beseech you!"

The Phantom spread its dark robe before him for a moment, like a wing. Withdrawing it, the Phantom revealed a room by daylight, where a mother waited with her children.

Soon the long-expected knock was heard. She hurried to the door and met her husband. On his careworn face was a look of subdued satisfaction.

He sat down to the dinner that had been waiting for him. Finally the woman asked, "Are we ruined?"

"No. There is hope yet, Caroline."

"If *he* will wait," she said, "there is."

"He is past waiting," said her husband. "He is dead."

Although she was a kind and forgiving woman, she was thankful to hear it. She said so, with clasped hands. She was sorry the next moment, and prayed for forgiveness.

"To whom will our debt be transferred?"

"I don't know. But by then, we shall have the money. We may sleep tonight with light hearts, Caroline!"

Even the children's faces, as they clustered round to hear what they so little understood, were brighter. The only emotion caused by the death was one of pleasure. It was a happier house for this man's death!

"Let me see some tenderness connected with this death," said Scrooge. "Otherwise, that dark chamber will be forever present to me."

The Ghost led him through several familiar streets. They entered poor Bob Cratchit's house. The mother and the children were seated round the fire.

Quiet. Very quiet. The noisy little Cratchits were as still as statues, and sat looking up at Peter, who was reading. The mother and her daughters were sewing. The mother laid her work upon the table and wondered aloud where her husband was.

"I think he has walked a little slower than normal these last few evenings, Mother," said Peter.

They were very quiet again. At last she said, and in a steady, cheerful voice, that only faltered once, "I have known him walk with—I have known him walk with Tiny Tim upon his shoulder, very fast indeed."

"And so have I," cried Peter. "Often."

"And so have I!" exclaimed another. So had all.

"But he was very light to carry," she resumed, "and his father loved him so, that it was no trouble. There's your father at the door!"

She hurried out to meet him. Bob came in. His tea was ready, and everyone competed to serve it to him. Then the two young Cratchits sat upon his knees. Each child laid a little cheek against his face to comfort him.

Bob looked at the sewing upon the table, and praised the hard work and speed of Mrs. Cratchit and the girls. They would be done long before Sunday, he said.

"Sunday! You went today, then, Robert?" said his wife.

"Yes, my dear," returned Bob. "I wish you could have gone. It would have done you good to see how green a place it is. But you'll see it often. I promised him that I would walk there every Sunday. My little, little child!" cried Bob. "My little child!"

He broke down all at once. He left the room and went upstairs, to a room hung with Christmas decorations. There was a chair set close beside the dead child's bed. Poor Bob sat down. When he had calmed himself, he kissed the little face. He accepted what had happened, and went downstairs again.

They sat before the fire and talked. "I am sure none of us will forget poor Tiny Tim," Bob said.

"Never, Father!" they all cried.

Mrs. Cratchit kissed him, his daughters kissed him, the two young Cratchits kissed him, and Peter and himself shook hands. Spirit of Tiny Tim, you are now with God!

"Specter," said Scrooge, "something tells me that we will soon part. Tell me—what man did we see lying dead?"

The Ghost of Christmas Yet To Come led Scrooge to a churchyard with an iron gate. The yard was overrun by grass and weeds. The Spirit pointed to one grave, and Scrooge went toward it, trembling.

"Before I draw nearer to that stone to which you point," said Scrooge, "answer one question. Are these the shadows of the things that Will be, or are they only shadows of things that May be?"

Still the Ghost pointed to the grave.

"Men's actions will lead to certain ends," said Scrooge. "But if the actions are changed, the ends will change. Say it is so!"

The Spirit was as silent and immovable as ever.

Scrooge crept toward the grave, trembling as he went. Following the finger, he read upon the stone of the neglected grave—"EBENEZER SCROOGE."

"Am *I* that man who lay upon the bed?" he cried, upon his knees.

The finger pointed from the grave to him, and back again.

"No, Spirit! Oh no, no!"

The finger still pointed.

"Spirit!" he cried, tightly clutching its robe, "hear me! I am not the man I was. I will not be the man I would have been if these Ghosts had not visited me. Why show me this, if I am past all hope?"

For the first time, the hand appeared to shake.

"Good Spirit," he went on, as he fell upon the ground before it. "Assure me that I may change these shadows you have shown me, by altering my life!"

The kind hand trembled.

"I will honor Christmas in my heart, and try to keep it throughout the year. I will live in the Past, the Present, and the Future. I will not shut out their lessons. Oh, tell me I may erase the writing on this stone!"

In his agony, he caught the spectral hand. It sought to free itself, but he was strong, and held it. The Spirit, stronger yet, pushed him away.

As Scrooge lifted his hands in a final prayer, he saw the Phantom's hood and robe change. They shrank, collapsed, and dwindled down into a bedpost.

CHAPTER 5
The End of It

The bedpost was his own. The bed was his own; the room was his own. Best and happiest of all, the time before him was his own, to reform himself!

"I will live in the Past, the Present, and the Future!" Scrooge repeated, as he scrambled out of bed. "The Spirits of all Three shall strive within me. Oh Jacob Marley! Heaven and Christmastime be praised for this! I say it on my knees, old Jacob, on my knees!" His face was wet with tears.

"They are not torn down," cried Scrooge, folding one of his bed curtains in his arms. "They are here. I am here! I am as light as a feather. I am as happy as an angel. I am as merry as a schoolboy. A merry Christmas to everybody! A happy New Year to all the world!"

He had raced into the sitting room, and was now standing there, out of breath.

"There's the door by which the Ghost of Jacob Marley entered!" cried Scrooge. "There's the corner where the Ghost of Christmas Present sat! There's the window where I saw the wandering Spirits! It's all right, it's all true, it all happened. Ha, ha, ha!"

For a man who had been out of practice for

so many years, it was a splendid laugh.

"I don't know what day of the month it is!" said Scrooge. "I don't know how long I've been among the Spirits. I don't know anything. Hallo! Whoop!"

He ran to the window and opened it. He was greeted by golden sunlight and sweet fresh air. Church bells were ringing. Oh, glorious. Glorious!

"What's today?" cried Scrooge, calling downward to a boy in Sunday clothes.

"Today?" replied the boy. "Why, Christmas Day."

"It's Christmas Day!" said Scrooge to himself. "I haven't missed it. The Spirits have done it all in one night. They can do anything. Hallo, my fine fellow!"

"Hallo!" returned the boy.

"Do you know the poultry shop in the next street but one, at the corner?" Scrooge inquired.

"I should hope so," replied the lad.

"A remarkable boy!" said Scrooge. "Do you know whether they've sold the prize turkey that was hanging up there?"

"What, the one as big as me?" returned the boy.

"What a delightful boy!" said Scrooge. "Yes, my lad!"

"It's hanging there now," replied the boy.

"Is it?" said Scrooge. "Go and buy it and tell 'em to bring it here."

"I'll send it to Bob Cratchit's!" whispered Scrooge, rubbing his hands and shaking with a laugh. "He won't know who sent it. It's twice the size of Tiny Tim."

Scrooge went downstairs to open the street door when the poultry man arrived. As he stood there, the door knocker caught his eye.

"I shall love it as long as I live!" cried Scrooge, patting it with his hand. "I scarcely ever looked at it before. What an honest expression it has on its face! It's a wonderful door knocker!—Here's the turkey. Hallo! How are you! Merry Christmas!"

It was a huge turkey. "Why, it's impossible to carry that all the way to Bob Cratchit's," said Scrooge. "You must have a cab."

He laughed as he said this, as he paid for the turkey, as he paid for the cab, and as he paid the boy. Then he sat down breathless in his chair again, and laughed until he cried.

He dressed himself in his best clothes and went out into the streets. The people were by this time pouring forth, as he had seen them with the Ghost of Christmas Present. Scrooge regarded every one with a delighted smile. He looked so friendly that three or four good-humored fellows said, "Good morning, sir! A merry Christmas to you!" Scrooge said often afterward, that of all the sweet sounds he had ever heard, those were the sweetest.

He had not gone far, when he beheld the portly gentleman who had walked into his counting house the day before and said, "Scrooge and Marley's, I believe?"

"My dear sir," said Scrooge, quickening his pace, and taking the old gentleman by both his hands. "How do you do? I hope you succeeded yesterday. It was very kind of you. A merry Christmas to you, sir!"

"Mr. Scrooge?"

"Yes," said Scrooge. "That is my name. I fear it may not be pleasant to you. Allow me to ask your pardon. And will you have the goodness—" here Scrooge whispered in his ear.

"Lord bless me!" cried the gentleman, as if his breath were gone. "My dear Mr. Scrooge, are you serious?"

"If you please," said Scrooge. "Not a farthing less. A great many back payments are included in it, I assure you. Will you do me that favor?"

"My dear sir," said the other, shaking hands with him. "I don't know what to say to such generosity."

"Don't say anything, please," retorted Scrooge. "Come and see me. Will you come and see me?"

"I will!" cried the old gentleman.

"I am much obliged to you. I thank you fifty times. Bless you!"

He went to church and walked about the streets. He watched the people hurrying to and fro, and looked into windows, and patted children on the head, and spoke to beggars. He had never dreamed that any walk—that anything—could give him so much happiness.

In the afternoon he turned his steps toward his nephew's house. He passed the door a dozen times, before he had the courage to knock. Finally he did.

"Is your master at home, my dear?" said Scrooge to the servant girl.

"Yes, sir."

"Where is he, my love?" said Scrooge.

"He's in the dining room, sir, along with mistress. I'll show you upstairs, if you please."

"Thank you," said Scrooge.

When Scrooge entered the room, his nephew Fred cried out, "Why bless my soul! Who's that?"

"It's I. Your Uncle Scrooge. I have come to dinner. Will you let me in, Fred?"

Let him in! It is a mercy Fred didn't shake his hand off. Fred's wife was equally enthusiastic. So was everyone who arrived. Wonderful party, wonderful happiness!

Next morning Scrooge went to the office early, so he could catch Bob Cratchit coming late.

The clock struck nine. No Bob. A quarter past. No Bob. Scrooge sat with his door wide open, that he might see him come into the office.

Cratchit was eighteen and a half minutes late. His hat was off before he opened the door; his coat, too. He raced to his stool and starting writing furiously, as if he were trying to overtake nine o'clock.

"Hallo!" growled Scrooge, in his accustomed voice, as near as he could fake it. "What do you mean by coming here at this time of day?"

"I am very sorry, sir," said Bob. "I *am* behind my time."

"Yes, I think you are. Step this way, if you please."

"It's only once a year, sir," pleaded Bob. "It shall not be repeated. I was making rather merry yesterday, sir."

"Now, I'll tell you what, my friend," said Scrooge, "I am not going to stand this sort of thing any longer. And therefore," he continued, leaping from his stool, "I am going to raise your salary! A merry Christmas, Bob!" said Scrooge, with an earnestness that could not be mistaken. "A merrier Christmas, Bob, my good fellow, than I have given you for many a year! I'll raise your salary, and I'll assist your struggling family. We will discuss your affairs this very afternoon!

Make up the fires, and buy another load of coal before you do another thing."

Scrooge was better than his word. He did it all, and much more. To Tiny Tim, who did NOT die, he was a second father. He became as good a friend, as good a master, and as good a man as ever lived. Some people laughed to see the change in him, but he let them laugh. He was wise enough to know that nothing ever happened, for good, at which some people did not laugh at first.

He had no further dealings with Spirits. It was always said of him, thereafter, that he knew how to keep Christmas as well as any man. May that be truly said of all of us! And so, as Tiny Tim observed, God Bless Us, Every One!

AFTERWORD

"Laughter and chills?" you might have asked yourself when you first saw this book's title. "What kind of a combination is that? Are these stories funny, or are they scary?"

Well, the answer is yes and yes—they *are* funny or scary. Some are only funny; some are just scary; several are both at once.

When you think about it, there is a long tradition of combining things that are scary and amusing. For instance, imagine yourself going through a "Haunted House" ride at a carnival. You're sitting in a cramped little car, rumbling along on miniature train tracks, and you enter a passageway that's as dark as the inside of a coffin. You hear a moan off to one side; something brushes your cheek lightly. You *know* it's all fake, and yet you're holding your breath with tension. Suddenly, a flash of light illuminates the outstretched arms of a crazed, bloody-faced zombie, lunging right toward you! You jerk away, shrieking in terror—and then burst into nervous, relieved laughter. Gotcha!

Moviemakers understand the link between fear and laughter. Alfred Hitchcock, the granddaddy of all horror filmmakers, was famous for inserting comic touches into his frightening films. In *Frenzy*, for instance, a movie about a serial killer, one scene shows a politician at an outdoor rally, lecturing the audience about pollution in London's famous Thames River. The camera shifts a bit and we viewers see that river—with a body floating in it. This is not the kind of "water pollution" the politician was thinking of. But our reaction? We gasp, then giggle. Later in the same movie, the killer realizes that his latest victim died clutching his tie pin, which could be used to identify him. He returns to retrieve the pin, which is trapped in the dead woman's rigid hand. He has to pry her stiff fingers open, and as they seem at the point of breaking—Snap! The scene shifts to a crisp breadstick breaking in half, as the police inspector on the case enjoys his dinner. Again, we shudder and laugh all at the same time.

In the case of the seven stories in this book,

let's look at how the funny moments and the scary ones stack up against one another. In "The Storyteller," the short-story writer known as Saki (his real name was H.H. Munro) does an amusing job of describing the boring aunt telling her restless nieces and nephew a very proper, very moral story. The children's loud questions and their lack of attention soon make it clear that they find the story deadly dull—and who wouldn't? And so here comes a stranger offering to tell *his* story. At first the story seems just as dull and moral as the aunt's. But then comes the twist. The stranger's story becomes a truly horrifying little tale in which the perfect little girl is eaten alive by a wolf—actually punished with death for being so good! Naturally, the children are delighted. What kid doesn't enjoy a gruesome story? Equally naturally, the stuffy aunt is horrified, and her scandalized reaction makes us laugh.

In "The Open Window," another story by the same author, Saki again demonstrates a taste for mixing humor and horror. As the young woman begins to tell her tale, we believe we are reading a tragic story. Then it seems to become a ghost story! And finally, the story's last lines let us in on the joke: we've been reading a comic story all along.

"The Ransom of Red Chief" is probably the most straight-out funny story in the book.

Although the plot revolves around kidnapping, which is certainly not a funny topic, we readers quickly realize that this is not a serious crime story. The kidnappers are obviously too soft-hearted (and maybe softheaded!) to hurt a fly, much less a child. We chuckle as the tables are turned on the criminals by terrible ten-year-old Red Chief.

No book of scary stories would be complete without a contribution from Edgar Allan Poe, and this has two: "The Cask of Amontillado" and "The Tell-Tale Heart." Poe is probably the world's best-known author of tales of the macabre. Pronounced *"ma kab,"* macabre is a French word meaning "having death as a subject." Like other stories that Poe wrote, the ones you'll find in this book give the reader a chilling glimpse into the workings of a mad, murderous mind.

On a much lighter note, we have "The Legend of Sleepy Hollow" which has been a favorite since its publication in 1819. In Ichabod Crane we meet a wonderful character: silly and cowardly, but at the same time puffed up with self-satisfaction. And he has a fatal weakness—he is highly superstitious. Just what happens to Ichabod is never fully explained, but generations of readers have enjoyed drawing their own conclusions!

Finally, there is Charles Dickens' masterpiece, "A Christmas Carol." What writer has ever brought together a less likable character (the hateful, miserly Ebenezer Scrooge), a more awful ghost (Jacob Marley, bound with his heavy chains), a more heart-tugging little boy (Tiny Tim, with his famous line, "God bless us, every one!") and tied them together in such a satisfying, finally joyous story—with plenty of shivers along the way.

Misers, kidnappers, schoolmasters, and murderers; open windows, train trips, headless horsemen and madmen; giggles and guffaws and shudders and shrieks—they're all here for your enjoyment. Have some frightful fun with *Laughter and Chills*!

If you liked
Laughter and Chills: Seven Great Stories,
you might be interested in other books
in the Townsend Library.

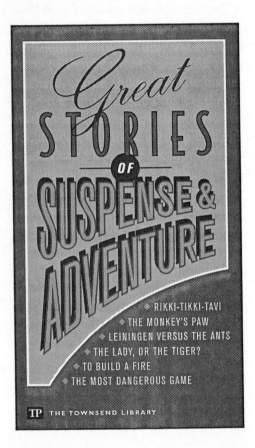

Great
STORIES
OF
SUSPENSE &
ADVENTURE

♦ RIKKI-TIKKI-TAVI
♦ THE MONKEY'S PAW
♦ LEININGEN VERSUS THE ANTS
♦ THE LADY, OR THE TIGER?
♦ TO BUILD A FIRE
♦ THE MOST DANGEROUS GAME

TP THE TOWNSEND LIBRARY